# The Boswells Connection

## STORIES LINKED TO OXFORD'S OLDEST STORE

Edited by

ANDREW BAX

*To Richard,*
*with best wishes*

*Geoffrey*

*Neil Harcourt*

*Geoff Brantley*

UPFRONT
PUBLISHING

## *The Boswells Connection*

Copyright © Andrew Bax, 2019

A CIP catalogue record for this book is available from the British Library

ISBN 978-178456-642-5

First published 2019 by Bombus Books
15 Henleys Lane, Drayton OX14 4HU
www.bombusbooks.co.uk

An environmentally friendly book printed and bound in England
by www.printondemand-worldwide.com

# Contents

Introduction *Andrew Bax*     v

The Portmanteau Maker *Annie Winner*     1

Dawn on Broad Street *Andrew Bax*     11

Two Thinkers *Geoff Bremble*     17

For Old Time's Sake *Jenny Burrage*     25

Street Talk *Neil Hancox*     31

Unstrung *Karen Gray*     39

The Blue Scarf *Jackie Vickers*     51

Just Another Tuesday *Andrew Bax*     63

A Life in Luggage *Karen Gray*     67

Recovery *Annie Winner*     75

The Dressing Case *Jackie Vickers*     85

Downsize *Neil Hancox*     93

The Trouble with You *Karen Gray*     101

A Job with Prospects *Andrew Bax*     113

Off the Beaten Track *Annie Winner*     119

Shopping with Mother *Neil Hancox*     129

Oxford in the Time of Cholera *Jackie Vickers*     137

Coming Together? *Geoff Bremble*     147

A Change of Heart *Jenny Burrage*     157

# Introduction

## Andrew Bax

It was Annie who first suggested Boswells. With entrances on both Cornmarket and Broad Street, Boswells has been part of Oxford's fabric for nearly three centuries. It is so familiar to residents, students and visitors that it is surprising we hadn't thought of it before. We asked the management: 'Could we write a book of stories linked to Boswells and, if so, could you help us sell it?' We pointed to success with our previous books, all of which sold well and raised money for local charities.

The answer was immediate: 'Yes.' What's more, they opened their files, told us their history and suggested ideas. No wonder they have a reputation for such friendly, helpful service and that the loyalty of staff and customers lasts for years. And when we'd done the writing, they did the graphics and that fantastic cover design for us. Boswells is donating a percentage of its profits from the sale of this book to its Charity of the Year.

While nearly all these tales are fiction, there is an element of truth in many of them. For instance, Annie has used her imagination to add flesh to the hard, sad facts about Henry Boswell, grandson of Boswells' founder. Other stories, both historical and contemporary, are based on the Oxford which readers will recognise.

Originally it was intended that Jackie Vickers would be our editor, with help from me. She has done this before so asked, this time, for our roles to be reversed. I would therefore like to record my appreciation of Jackie's hard work and eye for detail, so essential before the publishing process can begin.

# The Portmanteau Maker

Documenting the life of Henry Boswell (1835-1897)
grandson of Boswells' founder

## Annie Winner

**Two of a number of letters found in the papers of Laetitia Thornton, daughter of Joseph Thornton, bookseller, Broad Street, written to her by Mary Ann Boswell over a period of two years**

*2 May 1862*

My Dearest Letty

How sad that you have left Oxford. We miss you and your company. Friday afternoons are so dull now that you are not a regular visitor.

Please write to me and let me know how you are getting on. I am so sorry that your affection for my brother Henry was not returned. He is a strange creature and works so hard in the shop. I know he cares very much for me and has always been very kind and considerate, soothing me when I fret over my affliction and encouraging me to do what I can. I often see him poring over his beloved botanical specimens with a magnifying glass and see the absorption in his expression and wonder whether he has any interest in anything else. Perhaps his mosses are a distraction from his cares and he has no time in his life for love. When dear Papa died so suddenly, it was burdensome for Henry to continue the business and act as father to us all.

I long to hear from you about life in Leamington Spa. Is your aunt kind and are your cousins good company? Oxford is very quiet.

My best love to you

Mary Ann Boswell

*23 October 1864*

My Dear Letty

I am so pleased to get your latest letter and to know that you will be returning to Oxford. Seeing you after so long will be such a pleasure. I saw your brother yesterday and he told me the good news, then your letter arrived this morning. I told Henry we are expecting you. Things are going well and he is less preoccupied with the business.

You write of your attachment to your cousin's friend. I am so pleased for you. I do not think I will ever marry as my affliction cannot be an attraction, but it gives me great joy to see others happily settled.

This is just a short note as I will soon see your smiling face.

With my love

Mary Ann Boswell

## *Extract from Jackson's Oxford Journal April 21 1868*

*Marriages*

On April 16, at St Martins in the Fields, London, by the Rev A.E. Northey, Mr Henry Boswell, of the Corn Market was married to Catherine Martha, relict of Mr. William Castle Lucy, of 3 Park Place, St Giles.

## *Extracts from Henry Boswell's Diary 1868–1890*

*26 September 1868*

A week ago, I discovered that Catherine is not five years older than me, as she had claimed, but over 20. I was looking for some papers in her desk drawer and found a letter from her mother marking her fortieth birthday with the date on it. When I questioned her about it she just shrugged and offered no explanation. Such a deception has smothered much of the affection I had previously felt for her. It was not so much the fact of her age. She is still a handsome woman whose person attracted me just as much as her fortune. It is more the suspicion that she used duplicitous means to entrap me. I remember that Mary Ann did gently try to dissuade me from marriage to her, but at the time the expansion of the business needed financing and Catherine had a sizeable portion from her two previous marriages.

I am finding the realisation that I cannot now trust Catherine very discomforting. How can I believe anything she says when she not only has deceived me but seems completely unaware and therefore unrepentant of the wrong she has done me?

### 23 October 1879

Yesterday we buried my beloved sister Mary Ann. It was a clear and crispy day, the breeze ruffled the black veils of the women in the party and I could not hold back my tears. How can I go on without her sympathetic and understanding ear, her loyalty and discretion? She was a delight to me all her life. I remember when she was born. I was 11 years old and enchanted by her tiny fingers, her alabaster skin that would suddenly flush and then pale.

When she left school, she started working in the shop with her sisters. She had always suffered from convulsions – every now and then her gaze would go vacant and she would twitch and fall. One day in the shop she had a severe seizure. She fell to the floor, foaming at the mouth, her whole body in spasm, biting her tongue and voiding. After that we agreed that she should no longer work in the shop, so she took charge of the accounts which duty she performed with exemplary skill and attention to detail until the final seizure.

How bravely she bore the falling sickness that eventually killed her, not only its physical manifestations but the exclusion from society her condition dictated. As the frequency of the seizures increased, so did the limits she imposed on herself.

I cannot write any more now. I am too overcome.

### 28 October 1879

Another sleepless night, with memories of my gentle sister invading my thoughts constantly. She was always someone I could turn to when I suffered my occasional periods of melancholy. She shared this tendency to sadness with me, unlike our siblings who were always a jovial lot, laughing and joking. Mary Ann and I didn't need to talk much, but were able somehow to console each other just by being together. When we did talk her quick grasp of difficulties and her sharp perceptions always helped me to make the decisions that have led to our present prosperity.

I've tried to sleep, but now sit with one candle in the back parlour, leaving Catherine snoring in our bedroom and try to write out my grief. Where else can I find the wisdom and good sense she was always so generous with? My other sisters are kind and loyal, and Eliza sometimes helps me with my botanical interests, but their understanding is superficial. My brothers pay little attention to the business and pursue their own lives. As for Catherine, her sloth and cunning leave me unable to trust her to do anything to assist me. It's all she can do to manage the servants and receive visits from her chattering friends.

I should have listened to Mary Ann, as I did on almost all the other occasions in life when I had to make serious decisions. Indeed, life might have been very different had I acted on her strong hints that her sweet friend Letty Thornton had feelings for me.

The sky is lightening. I must try to sleep.

*22 November 1886*
Tomorrow I will be invested with an honorary Master of Arts degree from the University of Oxford. How I wish Mary Ann was here to share my pride and delight in this honour.

For many years I have devoted most of my spare waking hours to the study of bryophytes and now, despite my meagre education and lowly occupation, my work has been recognised by the most distinguished men in the field.

Catherine could not muster an ounce of enthusiasm when I told her, just as when my book about Oxfordshire mosses was published, she took no interest in its positive reception.

My life has been devoted to the business during the day and mosses

4

and liverworts by night and on Sundays, not least because my home is not a sanctuary, but a cold and lonely place. Catherine is polite but distant and we are rarely in each other's company. We spend but little time in society. I find her friends superficial and frivolous and she finds mine pompous and serious. She has talked of separation but that would hardly be practical.

*14 August 1888*

Catherine was buried today. She had been ailing for several months. We were never reconciled, and indeed became more and more estranged over the years. I took to sleeping in one of the smaller bedrooms and we rarely encountered each other except at the meal times when we were both at home.

A matter of months ago she had what the doctor called a fit of apoplexy as a result of which she was unable to speak or move her limbs and so was confined to bed. I hired a nurse and made sure she was comfortable during her final weeks until a further fit carried her off. As she requested in her Will, she was buried with her mother and William Castle Lucy (her second husband). To my surprise she left legacies to my two sisters. I felt a twinge of remorse at this news. Perhaps I have treated her with more harshness than she deserved.

*18 March 1890*

I should be discreet in case I neglect to destroy my diaries before I die, but I have a new love. She is someone I have known for years but I never realised she harboured feelings for me. She is married but her husband abandoned her over five years ago and she has no knowledge of his whereabouts. I encountered her in the shop one day and she invited me to visit her at her home in Jericho. I have been going there every Saturday night ever since. What delight! I never thought I would find such happiness or feel so complete. Of course we cannot marry but it is not unknown in Oxford for men to visit their women companions. Many of them live a distance away in Boars Hill or Headington. I am fortunate that S. lives but a few streets away albeit in a tiny terraced house. Since Mary Ann died so long ago, I have lacked the companionship of a sympathetic and affectionate woman and I relish the rediscovery of that pleasure, although we both live in constant fear of discovery and cannot go about together.

Arthur Pearson has made me an offer for the shop. I am minded to accept as he is offering me a sufficient sum, and I can then devote more time to my other interests.

### 20 August 1890

Yesterday we set off for a walk on Port Meadow at dusk, thinking it would be a time of day when few would be about. It was a hot and sticky evening and we felt the need for some air. Who should we encounter but my sister Eliza out with her little dog. She did not acknowledge us but crossed the street and scurried off towards her house in Kingston Road. This afternoon Eliza paid me a visit in my house in the Woodstock Road. She asked me what I was doing with a 'woman like that'.

'A woman like what?' I replied

'Do you not know she sent her husband mad with her adventuring, until he could endure it no longer and left her,' she said. And more, much more. I am too distressed to finish this entry.

### Extract from the Petition for admission to the Warneford Hospital submitted by Eliza Letitia Boswell, spinster, of 82 Kingston Road, Oxford, 1895

Having led a thoroughly regular life, apart from an illicit relationship with a woman about five years ago, my brother first started to behave strangely about two years ago. He began to stray from his normal habits and his speech became slurred and hard to understand. He entertained delusions, for instance that the neighbours were banging drums, and that storms were brewing although the weather was fine, and his conversation

was rambling. According to his housekeeper Elizabeth Cole, he has been roaming round the house in the middle of the night. [1]

## *Extracts from medical notes 1895-1897*

### *11 June 1895*
On admission the patient was in bodily good health, but in a state of evident mental weakness, smiling foolishly, with poor articulation and defective memory for recent events.

---

1  WV/169(iii}: Reception Papers held in the Warneford Archive, Oxfordshire History Centre

*17 June 1895*
Expressed an extraordinary string of delusions.

*26 August 1895*
Showed signs of General Paralysis.

*I January 1896*
Has become almost helpless and has to be washed and dressed.

*I January 1897*
Is quite helpless and can hardly speak.[2]

*Henry Boswell died on 1 February 1897. The cause of death was given as General Paralysis of the Insane, due to 'overstudy'. He was buried with his sister Mary Ann Boswell in St Sepulchre's cemetery. Their gravestone can still be seen.*

*All the characters in this story really existed. The letters from Mary Ann to Laetitia Thornton and Henry's diary entries are entirely imaginary, but the extract from the petition from Eliza Boswell and from Henry's medical records while he was in the Warneford Hospital are real (thanks to John Hall for his help in finding these). There is also a reference to a sister who suffered from epilepsy. 'Overstudy' was probably offered as an explanation for GPI to spare the family's feelings.*

*The title (The Portmanteau Maker) reflects how Henry Boswell described his occupation in several census records, the last being in 1891. The story has been pieced together from several sources including A Brief History of St Sepulchre's Cemetery by the Oxford Family History Society; here are some other, intriguing facts about his rather sad life:*

- *His wife, Catherine, was buried with her previous husband and her mother – why? It is customary for spouses to be buried together.*

- *Henry was buried with his sister (18 years after her death). Perhaps they were particularly close.*

---

2   WV/154/vi: Case Book V Warneford Hospital Archive, Oxfordshire History Centre

- *Henry Boswell's book, The Mosses of Oxfordshire and the Neighbourhood of Oxford, was published 1872.*

- *In 1886 he was awarded an MA by the University of Oxford.*

- *His wife was 20 years older than him – unusual.*

- *He died of General Paralysis of the Insane, which is caused by syphilis. How did he get it?*

# Dawn on Broad Street

## Andrew Bax

Although largely vegetarian, the Dodoth people supplement their diet with the milk and blood of their cattle. It was the sort of titbit that my grandfather would drop into conversation throughout my childhood, leaving me spellbound. He was a big man, big in size and big in character and, looking back, I think there were times when I was closer to him than to my own parents.

These days I spend much of my time recalling his old stories. I can still remember every detail and the gruff way he would tell them, his pale blue eyes focused on some distant horizon. There's nothing worth remembering from my own life.

My earliest memories are of walking around the village with him. Going on safari, as he called it. In his imagination we were already back in Africa. If we saw cows he would say 'Buffalo ahead. Nasty temper. Don't look them in the eye and they'll leave us alone.' Magpies would be vultures indicating a kill nearby. Cats would usually be cheetah but occasionally leopard. We were on constant watch for deadly puff adders and if we sat on a bank for a rest, we would have to stamp the ground first to flush out scorpions.

Just thinking about those days makes me smile. It's good to have something to smile about. I don't mix much with the others but most of them have nothing to smile about anyway. Maybe I'm just lucky.

The Dodoth occupy part of a region which, in relatively recent times, Europeans decided to call Uganda. At the age of 22 my grandfather was dispatched to administer an area roughly the size of Wales. This must have been some time after the First World War; he had volunteered for the Greenjackets but by the time he was posted to France the show was nearly over. Still, the experience was enough to give him a taste for excitement.

Over the years I learned so much about his life in the bush, the people with whom he lived, the animals that were all around and the warm, wide skies he described so vividly that Uganda always had a fascination for me. It became my life's ambition to see Africa for myself but, needless to say, the nearest I got was a boozy weekend in Barcelona.

The Dodoth were entirely self-sufficient and had no concept of material possessions other than their cattle and their women. The small, long-horned cattle that somehow thrived in that arid area were the currency that bought prestige and, of course, wives. A man was judged entirely by the size, not the quality of his herd. Indeed, it made no difference that his cattle may be thin, old or diseased, it was numbers that counted, and each of them was named. Although cattle were often treated in ways we would consider cruel the Dodoth had a deep, emotional attachment to them. Occasionally my grandfather would emit a thin warbling noise. It was one of many love songs the Dodoth sang about their herds.

Cattle, and therefore wealth, was acquired in three ways. Most obviously the herd was expanded through constant breeding. If a man was lucky he would have daughters to sell; a girl who was young, attractive and of proven fertility could be exchanged for as many as 100 cattle. But the most prestigious way of acquiring cattle, and sometimes women, was by stealing them from neighbouring tribes.

The Dodoth were a warlike people. Men carried a spear at all times, otherwise they were entirely naked. Many bore the evidence of battle in vicious scars, usually to their arms and legs. Wounds to the head and torso were invariably fatal.

My grandfather was in charge of a corps of native police whose primary role was to suppress the habit of raiding neighbours. In order to convey a sense of dignity the police were made to wear khaki shirts and shorts but they absolutely refused to wear boots. They were issued with rifles which, in time of need, were used as cudgels because they could not be trusted with ammunition. Off-duty, they discarded their uniforms, took up their spears and were just as liable to join a raiding party as any other fit young man.

This made my grandfather roar with laughter. He was a man of boundless good humour and spoke as if my future was going to be just as fun-filled and exciting as his. He died a long time ago so he wouldn't have known how wrong he was, but the stories he left still see me through the tough times. Here's one about the Reverend Ambrose Parker:

In 1907 the Reverend Parker suddenly felt the call to abandon his comfortable living in Guildford together with the spiritual needs of his equally comfortable parishioners and take up the Cross in Africa. The Church Missionary Society told him about an abandoned mission in northern Uganda, promised to pray for him and to stay in touch. Armed only with his modest savings, an unquenchable zeal and absolutely no knowledge of what he was in for, he ventured forth.

When my grandfather met him, he had established a little church which, through the liberal dispensation of sacramental wine, was attended by a modest and largely dissolute congregation on Sundays. More successful was his mission school at which he taught English, reading, writing, arithmetic and English history. The Church Missionary Society had provided a few copies of a picture book of Bible stories in which all the characters had fair skin, blue eyes and spoke English. It was therefore assumed that God was an Englishman. Things started to unravel when he introduced 'The World about Us' to the curriculum, beginning with astronomy. His assertion that the Earth, moon and sun were but grains of sand in a vast, swirling universe was seen as evidence that he had, at last, gone completely mad. He had always been considered suspect but after that attendance began to dwindle rapidly.

Within a couple of years, he had succumbed to a malarial infection.

The Dodoth honoured his body with ancient rites which made no Christian reference, and buried him vertically, as was their custom. After he had gone his few converts quickly reverted to their instinctive fear of the witches, spirits and fetishes that haunted the Dodoth world.

Me? Nothing much to tell really. Why Sheila agreed to marry me I shall never know. We had two sons who left home as soon as they could, and I haven't seen them for years; they probably despise me. Every job I took seemed to bore me so I was always on the move, and my last employer went down the pan. I think it was that that finished me; everything became a blur and most days I didn't even get out of bed. Sheila did her best to help but then she became ill too. I managed to drag myself up to the JR and saw her wired up to machines that scared me. I don't remember much after that, although I know she died. Months later I was discharged from Littlemore and that scared me too but they wouldn't take me back. By then, of course, the house we rented in Marston had been repossessed. So here I am.

A full moon tonight. That reminds me of another of my grandfather's tales. Every night when there was a full moon there would be an eerie rumbling sound punctuated every now and then by a prolonged wailing; it seemed to come from a long way away. He later learned that it was a ritual dance involving most of the young Dodoth for miles around, with no adults present. In it, teenage boys crouched in a circle, shoulder to shoulder, stamping the ground rhythmically and bellowing in imitation of their cattle. The girls would be inside the circle, stamping too; at a signal from one of their number they would leap into the air, shrieking. The dance seemed to go on for a long time and would end in a frenzy of love-making. I was only about ten when I first heard this story and didn't fully understand what was happening, but it seemed jolly exciting all the same.

A light's just gone on in Balliol College. Someone's up early. Can't sleep I expect, like me. And my grandmother. She would always be up by 5.00am, nagging my grandfather to get up too. That's another thing

I remember from my childhood. She was always nagging him about something.

By all accounts, though, it was love at first sight. They met during one of my grandfather's periods of leave and before he returned to Uganda they were married. On their way to the matrimonial home they were bumping along an earthen road in a heavily-laden truck when a herd of elephants started to cross in front of them. My grandfather stopped and turned off the engine. There were some very young calves and their mothers were nervously protective. Suddenly a grisly old tusker charged, flapping its ears and trumpeting loudly. The truck wouldn't start but the tusker stopped a couple of yards short, threatening them until the herd had passed. My grandmother must have been terrified but the experience served to toughen her for life in that remote outpost of empire. On her own initiative and without any training, she went on to run a clinic for the local women.

Marriage among the Dodoth was a complicated affair. Although it was a strongly patriarchal society, the wishes of both parties were considered if they were of a similar age. Their respective fathers would negotiate the price, and each would then negotiate further with their extended families. Thus, several families might contribute to the total of, say, 60 cattle; likewise, the bride's father would be expected to share those cattle among his extended family. In this way the community was strongly bound by ties of marriage and wealth.

A hut would be built for the bride in her mother's compound in which she would live until she had two children of walking age. Only then would she move in to live with her husband. He, in the meantime, may well have begun the process for acquiring other wives.

The Dodoth showed great deference to age so if a marriage was proposed between a girl and an older man, the girl's feelings would be discounted provided the price was right. When a man died, his brothers were expected to take in the deceased's wives as well as his cattle so that they were provided for.

Here in Oxford it's getting lighter now and starting to rain.

Rain. They didn't get much of it in northern Uganda and when it failed it brought starvation and disaster to the Dodoth. Such food as was available was given mostly to the young, fit and to the cattle. It was then that the spirits of the ancestors roamed the land looking for the poor, old and sick to join them. This sequence of events was accepted as part of the natural order of things.

I would like my grandfather to come and spirit me away right now. Early mornings are the worst. I can feel every bone in my body and that pain deep inside is getting worse. Soon there will be people hurrying to work, taking care to avoid eye contact. Fine by me; I might see someone I used to know. I must try to get some sleep.

Suddenly its daylight and the door is being pushed against me. The nice Boswells lady passes me a cup of coffee. 'We'll be opening in ten minutes' she says.

Time to go.

# Two Thinkers

## Geoff Bremble

*8 June 1933, Oxford*

It was late morning and the professor had at last completed the final draft of the lecture he was to give at Rhodes House. He was staying in rooms in Christchurch and had developed the habit of taking a walk along Cornmarket Street at around midday. He was in the company of James Harvey who had been assigned by the University to look after his needs during his stay in Oxford. They were now in the first-floor restaurant in Boswells department store looking out onto Broad Street and across to Saint Mary Magdalen church. Over the last few days he had observed a rough looking man walking with a distinct limp towards him past the church and pulling a small trolley. Its contents were covered by a well-used tarpaulin and, strapped to the trolley, were a couple of long rods both of which had at one end some sort of net.

'James, see zat man down there, pulling zat trolley. He's been doing zat at ze same time each day we've been here. Any idea why?' the professor said in a deep guttural voice.

James Harvey leaned over and looked out, 'He's a fisherman on his way to the river. I know him, poor chap. He lost a leg in the Great War and has never really recovered from his ordeal. But nice enough.'

'I vould like to go and vatch him fishing. Vould zat be alright?'

'Well you've nothing fixed for the rest of today, so why not follow him. But don't disturb him or you might get a mouthful.'

'A mouthful? I don't understand.'

'You will when you get it,' laughed Mr Harvey standing up, 'quick, you had better go or you'll lose him.'

The professor went down the stairs out onto Broad Street and, from a distance, followed the man down George Street. After about ten minutes and having reached Hythe Bridge he paused for a few moments to take in the feverish activity on the Canal Wharf to his left. There were barges lined up on the canal waiting for their turn to offload their goods before turning round to make the return journey north. Further beyond he could see the outline of Castle Hill which he had visited a few days earlier. After a moment or two he continued over the bridge, crossing the canal and the river Isis. It was then that he nearly lost sight of the fisherman but, looking to the right, he spotted him 50 yards or so along Upper Fisher Row starting to set up his equipment for the task ahead. After about ten minutes the man was ready and seated on the river bank. The professor watched as he flicked the baited hook upstream before allowing it to float slowly back towards him only to flick it back up once more. Eventually a fish took a bite causing the line to tighten as it made attempts to escape. The fisherman, engrossed in what he was doing, quietly reeled his catch to the bank manoeuvring it into his catching net and then in to the holding net. He began to re-bait the hook and the professor, seeing his opportunity, stepped down from the bridge and walked towards him.

'Vhat fish is zat, sir?' he asked.

The fisherman, surprised by the presence of this stranger and the guttural sound of his voice, responded without turning his head.

'It's a bream,' he grunted.

'I see, and vhat next happens?'

'As you can see I'm baiting the hook and when that's done I'll start fishing again,' the fisherman informed him abruptly.

'How long you sit zere doing zat?'

'Depends on how I feel and how the river is running. Maybe up to six hours.'

'And you finish. Vhat happens to ze fish you catch?'

'All the small ones go back into the river and the bigger ones I take home to eat,' explained the fisherman, now clearly irritated, 'and who knows, next day I might catch one or two of the little 'uns again.'

'I see, but I zink it takes a lot of time for small reward.'

'Until you try fishing you wouldn't understand,' said the fisherman, becoming even more exasperated by the man's continuing questioning.

'Ja, you are right I don't really understand why you do it.'

'For the peace and quiet, it gives me and time to think about things. I think about what I'm going to do for the rest of the day and tomorrow and the next day and about anything else that takes my fancy. At the moment I'm thinking why is this man interrupting my fishing and where does he come from?' The fisherman paused then said, 'You're a German aren't you? Did you fight in the Great War?'

The professor, taken aback, took time to answer.

'Ja, I am a German and no, I didn't. I vas vork in a university and vas staying to continue my research. Besides I vas 35 years old when ze War started and I vas too old maybe. And as you ask me, I may ask you same. Did you fight?'

'Yes,' replied the fisherman in a voice that made it clear this conversation would go no further before returning his gaze to the river. It was a full minute before the professor made an attempt to get back to where they had been earlier.

'You ask me if I vas a German I vas going tell you zat I think ve have something in common. Zat is, I spend also my time thinking.'

The fisherman, surprised by this comment turned once again to look up at the stranger who now seemed somewhat familiar, but he couldn't think why.

'What do you mean? You spend your time thinking.'

'Just zat. I'm in science trying to understand how is ze universe.'

The fisherman looked at him, bemused at these words.

'But it was God who made the universe, wasn't it?' was all he could think to say.

The professor paused, searching how to respond so that this man might understand.

'Zat's a good question. It's not about how it came to be I am talking, it is about how it is now and how it may change. As for God I never have managed to persuade a churchman zat even if we humans need a belief in a God there are many questions in science zat cannot be answered by religion alone.'

The fisherman was at a loss about how to reply. It was then that the professor who, having looked at his watch, made to go.

'Vell, I think zat's enough philosophy for now and it's been nice to meeting you. But I'm not sure to fish is for me and, looking at ze time, I should let you get back to it? Vouldn't you agree?'

'Yes, I would, but first just answer one question for me. How come you're here in the middle of the day? You're obviously not on your way to work.'

'Vell in a way I am. I am to give a lecture to ze University in two days time and I'm taking a break so zat I can clear my head to make notes on vhat I am to say. Also, I worry about giving it in English.'

'Oh, what's the problem?'

'Two years ago I give three lectures at ze University. In ze first one I explained my idea of a theory called Relativity, then in ze next one, Cosmology and in ze last one, Developments in Relativity. I give them in German, my native language. I have a full audience for ze first lecture but over ze next two ze audience got smaller and smaller. I think it was because not many understand German and even fewer ze mathematics. Zis time I'm to give my lecture in English and I vould be most embarrassed if only a few people turned up because they thought it was to be in German.'

'Oh, I wouldn't worry, the University will make sure that people know that it's going to be in English,' the fisherman offered with a grin.

'Yes, I know zat may be true but there's one other thing. Complicated mathematics are most difficult to understand. I will have need of three blackboards at least. When I did ze earlier lectures I used two,' he then drifted off into an afterthought, 'I think they've kept one in your new Museum of Science in Broad Street. Goodness knows vhy.'

The fisherman, now somewhat bemused by this train of thought tried to help.

'Yes, I know where you mean. It's next door to the Sheldonian Theatre, but I've never been in there. Look, I'm sure they'll give you as many as you need, and if they don't, just tell them you won't give a lecture unless they do,' before continuing, 'I assume you get what you want in your own university, don't you?'

'No, not anymore.'

'Why not?' asked the fisherman.

'Until April I have a position at ze Technical University in Berlin.'

'What do you mean, until.'

'Vell unfortunately my appointment vas stopped without warning.'

It was at this moment that the fisherman took another strike and the professor watched, fascinated by his skill in bringing the fish to the river's bank.

'Vell done, vell done,' he shouted. The fisherman looked up surprised by the almost childish reaction of someone he was beginning to realise was a person of some stature. It was then that he remembered where he had seen him before.

'Didn't I see you outside the Sheldonian in Broad Street about two years ago, all dressed up. You were leading the procession. I was just coming out of the White Horse opposite. I've had few beers in that place down the years I can tell you. Those parades, they're something to do with giving people degrees for stuff they've done, aren't they?'

'Ja, I vas to get an honorary degree. It vas at ze same time as I gave those lectures I told you about earlier.'

'Well, there you are, they must think a lot about you. So you can relax, and even if you do mess it up nobody's going to say anything,' the fisherman responded.

The professor looked at him, somewhat surprised by the fisherman's casual attitude.

'Ja, Ja, I suppose so,' he replied, but before he could continue the fisherman blurted out,

'Hang on, you're not a Jew, are you?'

'Ja, I am.'

'Did you lose your job because of that bloke Hitler? I've just read in the papers something about him taking charge in Germany and it said he doesn't like Jews.'

'You're right, he doesn't. He hates with a vengeance.'

'But why would he sack you? After all he must know you're someone really important.'

The professor smiled at this compliment and at what he believed was the fisherman's naivety.

'Really important or no, he is vhy I've lost my position. He passed a law stopping all Jews from teaching in universities. In April zey started burning my books and all books written by Jews, as vell as those by many great writers who don't agree with their ideas. There's a bounty of $5000 on my head and a paper has published a list of enemies of the German people "not yet hanged" and my name is on it.'

The fisherman paused for a few seconds or so, grappling to take in this startling information.

'Do you have any family still there?' he asked quietly as the realisation came to him what this must mean to the man in front of him.

'No, thank God. My first vife and two sons are safe in Switzerland and Elisa, my second vife is with me.'

'So, what are you going to do?'

'Don't vorry, I've done it. I've just finished visiting America universities and when Elisa and I returned we landed in Antwerp. I went straight to ze German Consulate, handed in my passport and gave up my German citizenship.'

'That's unbelievable. So where are you going to live now and how can you travel with no passport?'

'Ze passport's no problem. I have a Swiss one, taken out years ago that I can use and ve've got a place in Belgium where ve can stay. After zis lecture I'll go there and work out vat next to do. I get offers from friends in America and also European universities including Oxford.'

'Well, if it was me I'd get as far away from Germany as possible and take up that American offer, you never know what that Hitler fellow might get up to next.'

'Ja, you're probably right.'

''Course I am, that's definitely your safest bet.'

'Alright, decision made,' responded the professor with a smile, 'and now I must really go.'

At which the fisherman held out an arm.

'Here help us get up. Pass me my crutch, it's over there. I want to stand with you and shake you by the hand,' said the fisherman.

As the professor helped him to his feet, he suddenly remembered what James Harvey had said about the man having lost his right leg and the reality of what he saw rendered him speechless.

'Served with the Ox & Bucks in the Great War. Lost it a week before the Armistice. Bit of a bugger about that. But I get by and the fishing helps take my mind off things.'

Moved by this revelation the professor responded, 'You must have terrible memories.'

'Yes, and as long as I live I shall remember the many hundreds of pals I left behind who weren't as lucky as I. And what have we got to show for it? Strikes every day. How are we expected to survive on no work and Germany on the rise? It seems like it was a waste of time. I don't want to believe this, but it looks like we might have to do it all over again.'

A silence descended on the two men only to be broken by the professor.

'I'm sorry you feel like zat but I quite understand. So, after ze Great War, what happened to you. You have a job, ja?'

'It was fine at first. I got fitted with a leg at Roehampton, that's a hospital about 60 miles from here in London, and the government offered training. But nothing worked out for me although I do get an army pension and, I'm lucky, I live with my father and brother. They both work in the car factory, so between us we can make ends meet. You don't need to worry about me and I'm sorry about my rant, at least I'm still in my home town. You've lost your home and country and your job.'

The professor took the fisherman's hand, 'I'll be alright. As I say before, I vas in ze University during zat terrible time working on my theories. In truth I'm a pacifist but I can see your bravery in war and now in peace. I have real pleasure to speak vith you and if I ever come back to Oxford I vill come down here and hope to see you again.'

The parting was suddenly interrupted by James Harvey approaching them in obvious haste.

'Professor Einstein! Thank goodness I've found you. The Vice-chancellor would like to talk to you about your lecture. We must hurry.'

'Vell, it looks like I am to be going back into ze real world,' said Professor Einstein winking at the fisherman and then asking 'You vould like to attend my lecture? You'd be most welcome. It's in Rhodes House in South Parks Road.'

'Thank you, I'll think about it,' was the response as they shook hands, both recognising that each in their own way would have many hurdles to overcome in the years ahead.

Two days later the fisherman made his way to Rhodes House standing on the opposite side of the road out of sight. He watched for the professor and was sure that he had turned his head looking for someone in the crowd before entering its portals. The fisherman then made his way to the river and, down the years, he became well known for his tales about the famous Professor. Nobody ever believed the tales he told but that didn't matter, he knew them to be true.

# For Old Time's Sake

## Jenny Burrage

'That's the third time I've asked you to pass the butter.' Linda glared at Bernard across the red and white checked tablecloth.

'I wish you wouldn't read at the table, Bernard. I've asked you so many times not to do it. It ruins everything I have to tell you.'

'Sorry, dear.' He passed the butter dish across the table and put his newspaper aside. In fact, he hadn't been reading. His eyes had simply glossed over the pages. He had other more important things on his mind. Yes indeed. It had all happened two days ago while he was on the computer.

Was Facebook, in reality, a kind of dating agency? Bernard decided it was and it was thrilling and wonderful and mind-blowing when he got a message from an old school friend, Mavis. Bernard was seventy and needed something or someone to spice up his life. Newly retired and down but definitely not out. That was Bernard.

Life with his wife Linda was so predictable. Children had gone away to lead their own lives and the two of them left with time to … do what? He'd given Online Mavis the old 'my wife doesn't understand me' bit (true according to Bernard) with the 'we lead separate lives now' (definitely not true. Linda made sure of that).

'Let's meet, darling Bernard,' Mavis had suggested. 'For old time's sake.' And so it was arranged. Bernard noticed an exciting new tremor in his lower body and was often to be heard humming or even singing in the shower and now here he was, whistling as he stacked the dish washer after their breakfast.

'You seem very happy,' said Linda.

He smiled. 'It's being with you so much these days, my dear.' Linda gave him a few extra jobs to do on the strength of that remark. She didn't know, of course, that he was meeting the delectable Mavis that very day.

After he had mowed the lawn and pruned the roses and ordered their Waitrose weekly shop online, dictated by Linda (she was computer illiterate), he decided he would have to invent something to tell her, and quickly. He could feel both guilt and excitement revving up inside him but the excitement was winning.

'Just off to meet George in The Three Feathers,' he lied. 'I'll get a sandwich while I'm there.'

Linda tut-tutted but it was his weekly agreed treat so she could hardly stop him.

As Bernard drove to Oxford to meet Mavis, he thought back to his school days. He and Mavis had kissed often but apart from a bit of fumbling, that was it. Tame by today's habits.

He could just picture her, small with cherry red cheeks, a mass of blonde curls tied back in a bouncing pony tail with bobbles and the smiliest mouth he'd ever seen. She was hockey captain, a cross country runner and bassoon player, a popular girl. He knew she'd gone to Manchester University but they'd lost touch after that. And then he'd met Linda at the local bird-spotting group, as he and his mates called the local youth club. She was a good looker back then.

The car had to swerve suddenly to avoid a cyclist. Concentrate, he told himself. He was taking Mavis out to lunch at Boswells and he planned to arrive early so he could greet her warmly.

As he sat in the 1738 Tea Room, specially chosen as a treat for Mavis, the waiter brought him the menu.

'I'm waiting for a friend,' Bernard told him. 'She will be joining me soon.' The waiter put a second menu on the table. Bernard scanned the menu and knew instantly he would choose the Steak & Organic Exeter Ale Pie. It sounded delicious. Mavis remembered Boswells from her school days and was delighted when Bernard suggested it.

His mind drifted back to Mavis. If this meeting went well, he could book a room at the Randolph next time. He didn't think Linda would allow him to spend a night away from home but there had to be a way round that. He would put on his thinking cap.

Mavis lived in Reading, not too far away, and she had told him she was divorced so no strings there. This could be a regular liaison. Liaison … dangerous liaison. He liked the sound of that. His life could be so different. Maybe they could meet at her place.

Of course! It suddenly came to him. Why hadn't he thought of that before? He would invent a new friend in Oxford. Archie, yes, Archie, someone he could have known at school, who wanted to meet regularly. He'd find an old school photo, one of those long horizontal ones showing the whole school. He would point out this Archie person to Linda. She went to a different school. Simple. She never wanted to meet his friends anyway, too busy with the house and interfering, sorry just taking an interest in the lives of their two children.

'Bernard, Bernard!'

He knew it was Mavis. He looked around but she was nowhere to be seen, only an elderly woman with greying hair and a stick. The woman tottered unsteadily over and as she got closer, he knew.

'Bernard!' she threw her arms around him, the abandoned stick clattering to the floor. 'You haven't changed one bit after more than fifty years!'

No, but you have, he thought with horror. No wonder she hadn't posted her picture on Facebook. His vision of the two of them writhing passionately in a hotel room had drifted away. Instantly. He stared at her. The red cheeks were the only parts of her that were still as he remembered. Wrinkles ran around her face like rivers on a map, the grey hair was cut in a short bob, and her clothes were grey as well. She was plump now with bulges here and there under the greyness. The scarlet lipsticked mouth was incongruous, like a red traffic light in a cloudy sky. He couldn't speak.

Mavis slumped untidily into the chair opposite. She pointed to the stick.

'Hip replacement,' she told him, 'three months ago. Stopped me playing in the seniors' hockey team. Soon be back to normal.'

Bernard had a horrible picture of this fat little woman brandishing a hockey stick with a bunch of old girls like herself.

'You haven't spoken, Bernard,' she accused. She guessed he was overcome with emotion at seeing her again. 'Anything wrong?'

Bernard was getting an expert at not telling the truth.

'I'm not feeling too well, Mavis, but I came here as arranged so as not to disappoint you. I shall have to leave as soon as the meal is over.' Best not to prolong the agony, he decided.

Mavis hobbled round the chair and planted ruby kisses on Bernard's lips and cheeks. He froze. A blackness had descended on him and squashed away the excitement of the morning.

'Poor darling,' she said. 'Of course I understand. No matter. We can meet again soon, can't we?' She picked up the menu.

'I'll have Smoked Ham Quiche and a glass of Sparkling Chardonnay,' she said.


Back home, Linda was surprised to hear the doorbell. The Waitrose order wasn't expected until next day. It was a smiling George.

'Is his lordship in?' asked George.

Linda blinked. 'No, he's with you. At least that's where he said he was going. The Three Feathers.'

'No way. That's Wednesday. He's made a mistake.'

'Silly old Bernard,' said Linda with gritted teeth.

'Must have been a senior moment, eh Linda? I came round to see if he fancied coming with me for a game of snooker.'

Linda wasn't listening. He's got a woman. That must be it, or why the secrecy? No wonder he's been so cheerful. She knew now why he'd been wearing his best cashmere jumper she'd bought him for his birthday. She clenched her hands. She might have known he was up to something.

'Would you like a cup of tea and a piece of my fruit cake, George?' she asked. 'Bernard will be back soon, I expect, and he'll be so pleased to see you.'

The key in the lock could be heard as George was finishing his second piece of cake and in walked Bernard. There was a stony silence. Thankfully the lipstick stains on Bernard's mouth had been eaten away. Unfortunately, two lipstick imprints remained, one on each of his cheeks, making him resemble a startled clown.

George stared at Bernard.

'Your wife makes lovely cakes,' he said.

# Street Talk

## Neil Hancox

'Hello! I am Broad Street or, if you are fussy the voice of Broad Street. Streets are a skin of stones, tar and asphalt atop a foundation; underneath are lots of tubes, wires, pipes and even sewers. If you think about it, we are similar to a human body in some ways. We have a good sense of what is happening 'up above' and we 'talk' to one another. I am not going to tell you how we do that. I don't intend to give away our secrets just entertain and, I hope, educate you a little. The name Broad Street has a good ring to it, though Squat or Sturdy would have been a more accurate and alliterative name.'

'You people take us all for granted, walk all over us and complain about traffic, pot holes and rubbish in the gutters. You never say thank you to us for making your journey possible. Neither for that matter do bicycles, cars, vans or lorries which scoot along or crawl all over our surfaces.'

'Now I have that off my chest I'll fill you in on a bit of my geography. I run, not literally of course, roughly west to east. I'm narrow at the Cornmarket, or west end, by Boswells – an excellent all-round department store and one of Oxford's oldest establishments dating from the earlier part of the eighteenth century. I'm proud that it has two entrances on my patch. Poor Cornmarket, off to the south, it's a bit grumpy because it has been dug up and specially resurfaced several times in the last few years, all to please the council.'

Cornmarket coughs to attract attention. 'I'll remind you I too have an entrance to Boswells and I have acquired bollards at either end which ups my profile a bit, don't you forget that,' he says.

'OK, I had better move on. There are two more streets meeting at the cross roads at my western end.' One of them, George Street, which goes on westwards towards the bus station, 'chips in.'

'I call it Boswells corner. And don't forget Beaumont Street,' he adds.

'None of us can,' I say. 'He's been unbearable since that book was published about him. What was the title, It Happened in Beaumont Street? Something like that. Totally gone to his head, thinks it's Beaumont Street and others.'

'Don't forget us either,' a northern voice pipes up. I smile. 'Of course not, Magdalene Street and your twin Magdalene Street East. I might add, on the quiet, that the latter is stubby and more of a bus park.'

'Phew! I am going to leave the city end and go east. I broaden out to host much sought after car parking space, where there were once houses centuries ago, before I narrow down again to another cross roads where I meet Parks Road, Holywell Street, which isn't particularly holy as far as I know, and Catte Street.' I whisper the last name. 'She can be very bitchy if you rub her up the wrong way. I think that the lack of a Dogge Street shows the poverty of imagination of the city fathers. That's another point to ponder; why don't we have city mothers? They would probably make a better job of things. You see I am modern, not stuck in past centuries. I've had plenty of time to think these things through; so have people but they can be so stupid.'

'Would you be quiet a minute,' Parks Road interrupts. 'Tell them that I am academic, not trade.'

'Of course, I'll make sure everyone knows that. He's not too bad really. I think it's being a road that is the problem although today the class barriers are eroding.'

'I am home,' you know, 'to bicycles, parked, propped and pedalled and crocodiles of tourists. You used to be able to identify Americans by their solid shoes with indented and patterned toe caps and the prevalence of plastic hoods at the first intimation of rain. Now it's Chinese, Japanese, trainers for all and selfie sticks for most. Then there are noisy kids learning English, that's the idea anyway, rough sleepers; touts, conmen (and why not con-women?). College students pour forth onto my surface, shouting and laughing, sad, lovesick, indifferent. Visitors sit at tables outside pavement cafes, though these establishments come and go, something to do with the economic outlook, I believe, as well as the weather, or leave my broad expanse to go into different incarnations of Blackwell's bookshops, the Weston Library, the Science Museum (really old stuff, but I suppose that's what you get in museums) or The Sheldonian. My advice to anyone going to a concert there is to take a cushion. Otherwise you will have a more permanent impression of events than you imagined.'

'He's on a rant again, proper little proletarian pile of stones,' the shrill voice of Queen Street reverberates. 'Perhaps we should ask the council to give him a soap box.'

'That annoys me. You can talk,' I say to her, 'currying favour with the new Westgate Centre.'

'Now, now, all you roads and streets, calm down.' The tone is firm. St Aldates, always reasonable and conciliatory, has spoken. 'I suppose that's why he has the Town Hall and the Crown Court.'

'I think, Broad Street,' he continues, 'you should adopt a couple of tourists for a few hours and guide them down your length, tell them about events, show them some shops, look after them.'

St Aldates has commanded. I calm down, settle on a middle-aged man and woman outside Balliol and listen in to their conversation.

'Where are we Herbie?'

The broad-shouldered man adjusts his baseball cap and pushes his fingers into the front pocket of his shirt. He extracts a $5 bill, a twenty and some coins. Finally, he finds a map of Oxford City centre, courtesy of the tour company. A thumb nail underlines Broad Street.

'Here we are Con,' he says.

A few minutes later the couple have stopped at an official notice board, between the entrances to Balliol and Trinity bearing the imprimatur City of Oxford, so it must be correct.

'It says here,' Herbie tells his wife, 'that Broad Street goes back to the 13th century. I expect it was just a track then.' He likes to add his own opinion to anything official.

His wife digests the information. After a moment's thought, and being of a sound biblical upbringing, she quips, 'that's as old as Methuselah.' I nudge the man in my own special way. He rubs his ear and then extracts another leaflet from a pocket.

'There is a stone cross let into the centre of the street here,' he points as he speaks to Con. 'It commemorates the spot where three religious martyrs were burnt to death in the middle of the 16th century.'

Con shudders. 'How horrible. What had they done?'

Herbie reads on. 'They were high ranking Protestant clerics, Cranmer, Ridley and Latimer. It's religious niceties. They had some slightly different views on God from the official line and if you didn't love God in the right way you were in trouble. Sort of make an example of a few to stop the rot.'

They are both silent for a minute or two.

My couple move on, crossing to my other side. They sample some fudge, and are now happily embedded in their seats, at one of those small pavement cafes I mentioned, coffee and croissants on their table. They are taking an interest in the crowds of people walking up and down, round and across, standing, gossiping, looking at maps, consulting mobile phones and ipads.

'I've been thinking, Con,' Herbie says in his precise analytical tone. Con groans inwardly. Herbie thinking is a sign of trouble, tangential trouble. He continues, 'why not follow M. Laplace, the 18th century mathematician, and consider everyone here, at this moment, as a fundamental unit. If I know everyone's position and velocity, now, I could predict what would happen thereafter.'

Con slips her tongue below the foam on her cappuccino, finds the liquid too hot and bites into her croissant, which is rather tough. Perhaps she should dip the pastry into the coffee and thereby render them both palatable? Herbie, her beloved Herbie, of 37 years of partnership, occasionally has these strange deviations.

She smiles at him. 'Remember you have often told me that at the fundamental level the world is not deterministic, even if Professor Einstein always maintained that 'The Old One' does not play dice.'

Herbie's foray into the mathematical future slowly decays.

Fortunately, a diversion is at hand. The next table is suddenly occupied by an elegant young woman, dark hair pressed close to her skull, her figure covered by a tight green satin dress.

'Herbie, what are you doing? Stop gazing, and she is awash with daddy cash,' Con adds in a waspish aside.

A young man appears, fashionably dressed in dinner suit, white shirt, collar undone and a bow tie floating free. He has that haggard look of late nights, drink and overwork, a typical student, which is why some say that education is for the young. Older folk would probably succumb to exhaustion. (Indignant older folk, studying for a D Phil on the influence of Sanskrit on Virgil's use of the vocative case in the Aeneid, please protest to the editor.)

He approaches the elegant young woman. 'Hello,' he ventures and is greeted with a smile that stops in the lipstick at the corners of the mouth.

A stuttering desperate look appears in his eyes. He beckons for the waiter and begins speaking to her hesitatingly, 'I never had a chance to tell you last night, I'm reading PPE, that's…'

'I know,' the girl replies, 'pompous, precocious, exhibitionism.' Hard eyes probe him, reaching to the back of his head, hooking into the pain already there.

Herbie nudges his wife. 'You can hear the hiss of his escaping dignity,' he whispers.

He is a determined young man, though, and tries another line, the girl smiles, pushes back her designer sunglasses, leans across and kisses him on the cheek. They toss some coins on the table and leave hand in hand.

'What did he say?' Herbie asks his wife.

Con shakes her head. 'I don't know but that young man is sure heading for high political office one day.'

Their refreshments finished, I nudge Herbie and Con again. They still have plenty of ground to cover. Think I'll show them the Oxfam Shop. This is not any old charity shop and it has a blue plaque to reinforce the point. It was the first shop, and site of the original offices, of the worldwide charity Oxfam founded in Oxford in the aftermath of World War 2.

The couple look at the window display and read the latest disaster appeal. 'There's always a disaster natural or man-made somewhere,' Con comments. Her husband agrees.

The next window to catch their attention is Broad Canvas with its exciting display of paints, canvases and pastels. 'It makes me think I should try my hand at art,' Herbie says. His wife demurs. 'You might give Picasso a run for his money but he already has the reputation my dear.'

A bicycle, three tourists and a ubiquitous white van stop them as they are about to cross The Turl.

'Oh dear. I forgot to mention The Turl, which joins me up with High Street, when I was giving you my geographical details. Never mind. Good morning,' I say. The Turl nods, its mind clearly elsewhere. On its other side my couple stop to admire Blackwell's Art and Poster shop.

'Look,' Herbie exclaims, 'there she is.' He points to a picture of an angular girl dressed in a green satin dress. 'Tamara de Lempicka. Art Deco herself.'

The print is examined from several angles. 'There are similarities,' Con admits. 'But this was painted in the 1920s,' she squints, 'or 1930s.

That would make the girl we saw a hundred years old. There is something very odd happening here.'

Herbie, now in practical mood, tuts. 'There's nothing psychic,' he says, 'the girl's been to a fancy-dress party.'

'You are too serious, Herbie, 'I was only teasing,' she says. 'Let's cross over and have a look at Blackwell's main book shop.' She wants to go in, he is not so sure. Books are heavy. Maybe a paperback would be OK. They move on to the Weston Library, up the steps and into the cafe.

'This is very busy,' Herbie observes. 'Anyway, I need a proper drink, a pint of English ale. According to the guide book there's a pub nearby, The Kings Arms, we'll go in there. I might have real steak pie as well.'

Con feigns amazement. 'Herbie you are a registered Republican and that place has royal connotations.'

'You have to go with the spirit of the time and place,' he replies, completely missing her suppressed smile.

He stops. 'Have you occasionally been aware today of a buzzing in your ear or a gentle push on the side of your face or back of the neck?' he asks Con. 'It's as if somebody is trying to guide you where to go next.'

'And have you been taking your pills, my dear?' she counters.

'Of course.'

Con sighs. 'OK, I have heard a strange noise in my head now and then, as if someone was trying to speak to me, tell me things. I thought it was the all this sightseeing; that can be very tiring at times.'

'Nudges and noises in their heads, indeed. Well I suppose they would never believe that a mere street talked to them.'

Herbie pauses and adopts his magisterial pose. 'We both need to sit down and have a proper drink.'

'And a real steak pie,' Con adds.


I've seen two middle aged tourists safely from one of my ends to the other, shown them sights and people. I've done my bit or have I? Perhaps not.

I hear Con say, 'so far Herbie, we haven't bought any presents or mementoes of our visit to Oxford.'

Her husband wipes his mouth and finishes his glass of ale. He digs into his shirt pocket, a little wearily, and produces another leaflet. 'Don't know where I picked this up,' he says, 'but it says something about shopping in the city.' He hesitates. 'Is Oxford a city?'

'Oh, get on with it Herbie,' Con answers.

'It says,' he continues, 'that that Boswells department store, at the junction of Broad Street and Cornmarket, is a great source of presents and gifts.'

'How do we get there?' Con asks. I groan. I thought I had shown them my geography pretty well.

Herbie extracts his map. 'We walk back the way we have come until we arrive at a busy junction.'

I'm tired, so I'll trust them on this one, they should be able to make it on their own.

*Some shops and fixtures on Broad Street and the adjacent area come and go. When this story was written there were pavement cafes in Broad Street. So, if you visit and don't find any you'll have to come back a few months or a year or so later.*

# Unstrung

## Karen Gray

The door slammed behind me more violently than I meant it to. Then everything went quiet. Shockingly quiet after all the shouting. I stood alone outside the room, fighting for self-control. Then, deep breath, head up, I eased my shoulders into the straps of my violin case and headed through the hush of the carpeted hotel corridor to the lift.

Downstairs, the doorman followed me out onto the street.

'Taxi, Miss?'

I shook my head. 'I'm not going far.'

The streets of Oxford were busier than yesterday, congested with people and summer heat. Caravans of tourists, smart phones in their hands, blocked my way, eyes darting from their screens to the sights they had to tick off before they left. Many of them had the straight black hair, round face and olive-toned skin typical of the Chinese. Just like me. Except that I wasn't Chinese and I wasn't on holiday.

I needed to find my spot. Arriving at a corner I recognised the store where Mom had insisted we shop the day before. We were regular travellers these days, as demonstrated by the battered state of our luggage. I didn't mind that, it went with being a professional. Mom, being Mom, more independent than practical, had a habit of hauling her carry-on bag up and down airport steps by its telescopic handle. Deaf to offers of help and even deafer to my warnings, she had persisted until the handle gave up the ghost on the escalator at Heathrow and refused to tolerate any further abuse. A new one was needed. On my expense account, of course. The hotel receptionist gave us the name of a store. They said it was Oxford's oldest, well known for its range of suitcases and not far from the hotel, so the day after we arrived in Oxford she decided we would go and find 'Boswells & Co'. Such a cute name. And not difficult to spot as it was up there above the shop windows five times in two streets. Once Mom had found an unsuspecting sales assistant she could commandeer, and was happily wheeling bags up and down steps and around the ground floor, I decided to leave her to it and snuck off to explore.

Upstairs I found a café. 'Tea Room' they called it but I could smell the coffee. And toys. A lot of toys. Things I had not seen much of as a child and certainly had no use for now. I decided to bring Mom up here for a coffee. We both lived on coffee. But back down in luggage Mom was still wheeling cases up and down, so I carried on down into the basement. Here there was a whole bunch of homewares. Mostly for the kitchen. More stuff I had no use for. There were tools for stirring, whisking, flipping and beating. There were dishes for baking, pans for roasting and frying. What couldn't you prepare, cook and serve for your friends and family with equipment like this? I would never know. But I did know that Mom would be a long time yet, so I wandered round, feeling curiously out of my comfort zone with this domestic abundance.

'Can I help you with anything?' The sales assistant seemed concerned. I must have looked as lost as I felt.

'Excuse me?'

'That dish is perfect for lasagne, if that's what you're after?' I put it down hurriedly.

There are special dishes for lasagne?'

'Well, we once had a customer come in with sheets of her favourite brand of lasagne pasta to make sure it fitted properly. This is the one she bought.'

'Wow. Really?' I explained hurriedly that I didn't cook much. The assistant nodded.

'Are you a student? We have lots of them here buying their first kitchen equipment. I remember one young man who came back to complain that his casserole dish had blown up.' She waited for me to react. I didn't. She went on.

'He'd bought a Pyrex casserole, you see, and was trying to use it on a gas hob.' I drew a blank. Pyrex? What was Pyrex?

She gave me a sympathetic look.

'OK, just let me know if you need any help.'

I was playing with a thing for measuring spaghetti when Mom called me on her cell phone. She had the new carry-on bag that had passed all the tests but there was no time for coffee in the Tea Room. I had to go practice. Of course I did.

But, I reminded myself, that was yesterday, this is now. Time to pick that spot. I turned the corner round Boswells and walked up the street promising myself I would come back for the coffee when I had achieved my mission. Hitching my violin case higher on my back, I walked away from the bustle of shoppers as far as a theatre, the Sheldonian Theatre. Across the street, the bright blue-painted frontage of a bookstore drew my eye, several people just inside the door leafing through books. Maybe book readers would also be music lovers? Here, I felt a little more at home. Further on was a modern building, the Weston Library with its wide and welcoming steps. Would they make a natural stage for me? This part of the street was less about shopping, more about art, literature and contemplation. I backtracked a little, unsure. Between the Sheldonian and a building called the Museum of the History of Science I found a triangular space, set back from the sidewalk, with a path to a side gateway. This was cool. I could stand with the wall and railings at my back. Carved stone heads on top of pillars set between the railings stood guard above the wall. Here I felt safe. Let's do it.

I laid my violin case gently on the ground. It rocked slightly on the unevenness of the pebbles set into concrete. My fingers fumbled at the clasps although I must have undone them a million times. There's always this nervous excitement just before a performance. But that's OK. There's a sort of grounded confidence too, the gift of practice. As soon as I start to play, once the muscle memory kicks in and the glory of the music takes over, my nerves dissolve, like ice in a warm coke on a hot day. Mom had always instilled in me that it's good to be nervous before a performance, it means you are taking it seriously. She is right about that at least.

I wondered again what Mom was doing. I closed my eyes, trying to compose myself before taking my stand to play. Was she still in the hotel room? Did she stay there after we'd rowed and I'd slammed out of it? It was an okay room I suppose, plenty of space for the two of us, looking out from the front of the hotel. No back-of-the-building brick wall views for us these days. Since my career took off and my mother started to run things, she booked only the best.

In this room, our home for the week, there was every comfort. The dish of artfully prepared fresh fruit was replenished daily and the decorations were elegant, cool and coordinated.

In this room, there were no birthday cards propped on the mantelpiece. No crumpled newspapers on the coffee table, nor open magazines, nor abandoned mugs of half-drunk coffee. No biscuit crumbs scattered on the carpet. No coats on the backs of chairs. No letters with the envelopes ripped open, lying about for someone else to pick up. No music leaking through a bedroom door or smell of baking from the kitchen. No cushions contorted by the weight of the last person to lounge on the sofa. No scent of garden flowers thrust into a jug or a jam jar. No clothes abandoned on the bed, wardrobe door left gaping. No family photos recording birthdays, weddings, holidays in the sun, all pushed into random frames and marshalled together like a happy family army. No fridge doors covered with children's art. No sound nor smell nor touch nor look of home.

Was Mom still there? Waiting for her phone to ring? Wondering where I was?

I doubted it. One thing about Mom, she doesn't do a lot of waiting, or wondering. She's good at questions, though, you have to give her that. Like the day I came second in my first big competition at the age of 12. Right off she asked, 'Why didn't you come first?' And then there was the time when my name was getting known, but before I had a wider, like international, reputation, and she appointed herself my manager. I had been practising before and after school every day since the age of six. That was half my life till then. I started to get tired from doing so many concerts and performances. All I heard from her was, 'Don't you know these people pay good money to hear you play? You can't disappoint them! Think of your career!'

Only she didn't ask it, or say it. She shouted it.

That was how the row in the hotel had started. She had slipped another engagement into the diary for our stay in Oxford, some corporate function, a favour for a business contact she wanted to get on the right side of. I was to play at the reception. An award was being presented and they wanted to make an impression. There would be a bunch of people all dressed up, glasses of champagne, lonely little bits of fancy food spaced out on trays, and not one of the guests even looking at me, let alone listening to my playing. They would be too busy eating, drinking and making sure they were seen talking to all the right people. What was the point? I would be paid of course, but it was goodbye to our one free evening and I felt the stab of painful memories at the prospect. All those years of missing out on sleepovers and school trips, my childhood swallowed up in hours of practice at home, or being tutored by demanding, ill-tempered, white-haired ex-professionals because I was 'a natural'. My life had been anything but.

So that's when I flipped. I told her I'd show her that it wasn't always me, or the music that people came for. Even the concerts – they're part of the social season. You have to be seen to be cultured.

'Go on then, show me! Prove it!' Her voice stung me. She thought she was winning but I was ready. I hit back at her with my plan and stormed out. I don't know who was more surprised, me or her.

I hope I didn't break that door.

The carved heads above me in the street were waiting. It was time to take my stand and put my plan into action. I gathered together my drape of dark hair and twisted it into a loose knot on top of my head. Here begins the ritual. I always wash my hands before playing to protect the varnish on my fragile instrument, but there was no way I could do this in the street, so I take out my violin and kiss the scroll, just as I do every time I play. The body tucks in where it belongs, on my shoulder. With my chin on the rest, I lift my bow and play a few open strings, G, D, A, coaxing out the sound I want until I feel the resonance down my arm. Then I make the E string sing out. Finally, I take a deep breath and begin with Bach's Chaconne. I can immerse myself in this piece, forget my Mom, the rows, the reason I'm here. My violin and I are one fused being. Here we go.

I play on, losing track of time until I decide to finish with Paganini's Caprice 24. Sure it's ambitious but I want to finish with a bang. A minute and a half of fireworks to prove my point. I'm in full flow, buoyed by the power of the sound emanating from the lungs of my violin. The fury of the music wraps around me like a fierce hug.

And guess what. No one took the slightest bit of notice. Cars slid past me, bicycles, buses and vans. The sun sidled across the sky. People strolled. People hurried. Nobody stopped to listen.

There was one guy though. He was sitting further along the street, on a ledge at the base of the wall that ran round the outside of the Sheldonian. He didn't really look like he was listening, he'd taken refuge inside the hood of his sweatshirt. I'd say he was younger than me, but not by much. Late teens, early twenties maybe. Tight jeans, arms crossed over a skinny chest. One plimsolled foot was hooked through the strap of a sagging black rucksack on the floor beside him. I reached the climax of the Caprice, and dropped my aching arms. I sure wish I had thought to bring a bottle of water from the hotel, then I realised I had come out without any money. Just my phone and my violin. How dumb was that? The guy strolled over, he was taller than I thought. Rucksack over one shoulder. Hands in his pockets. Definitely early twenties now I could see his face.

'You're good.' So he was listening.

'I practice.'

'How long for?'

'All day.'

'Since when?'

'Always.' He nodded and turned away.

'Do you play?' I asked. It felt important to know. He laughed.

'Me? No way!' He looked down. 'So where's your hat?'

I touched my bowing hand to my head. 'Hat? What hat?'

'Most buskers put a hat or something down here.' He tapped his foot on the cobbles in front of me. 'You know, to collect the money.'

'Oh, I get it. No, I'm not playing for money.' The hood was pushed back and he stared at me.

'So why are you doing it?'

We had talked for some time when he offered to go and buy me a coffee while I had a break, bringing me back a cappuccino in a cardboard cup. He'd accepted my explanation about playing to win a bet without comment and laughed when he heard that I didn't even have the price of a coffee on me. While I drank, I learned that he had grown up in Oxford, grown up with that toy department I had seen in Boswells, and had worked there as a university student during the vacations. He had a degree in English and wanted to work in publishing but had not landed a job yet. Surely, he would find something soon? Had he tried any other field? He countered all my questions with some of his own. I told him about the constant travelling and performing, the downside of living in hotels, and about that lucrative but pointless performance that I didn't want to do. I told him about the row it had caused with Mom and the challenge she had set me. Or had I set it myself? By then he'd gone quiet so I finished the coffee and took up my bow again. Taking the hint, he went back to his seat on the wall.

He was still there half an hour later when I lowered my bow after a second burst of playing. Again, there had been no audience, nothing to distract me, not even a rustle of applause, but a little girl was standing close by, her hands pressed against each other as if she were praying. When she caught my eye she clapped them together, like mini symbols.

'Play something for me!'

I shook my head, 'Not right now, I need a rest.'

She hung her head and bit her lip. I bit mine too. That was mean of me. A woman stepped forward.

'Sorry, we didn't mean to bother you. It's just that it's her birthday today. We've come shopping so that she can spend her birthday money.' She gave the little girl a gentle push. 'Show the lady, Claire.'

The girl thrust her wrist out. Fastened safely round it was a small zipped pouch on a band fastened with Velcro. It was patterned, pink and sparkly. She shook her arm so that the coins chinked inside. I thought how I never had any money of my own these days, everything was taken care of for me. Just like the British Queen here, so they say. I took up my bow again and played Happy Birthday, ending with a few exaggerated flourishes to make her smile. And she did, big-time.

'What's your name?' she asked.

'Rebecca.'

'Mine's Claire!' Proud grin. 'Rebecca what?'

'Yeo.'

'Yo?'

'Y-E-O. Yeo, yes.'

For once there was no reaction. No lifted eyebrow at my American accent and Asian looks. No need to explain that my American father had met my mother in Singapore, that they had later married and moved to the States where my sister and I were born.

Instead: 'Can we do a selfie? Oh please, Mum?' The girl put her hands together again, pleading. The woman hesitated, then got a phone out of her bag. What could I do? I caved.

'Sure thing,' I said.

'I want to hold it!' Claire grabbed the phone. I'm not the tallest, but it was clear that the little girl was way too small to hold the phone up high enough. Her mother said she would take the photo but there was no question the girl was going to let her. By now I just wanted to get back to the hotel, but there was something about her determination, her budding independence that I totally got.

'Wait,' I said, 'Come here.'

I guess I was still trying to make it up to her, so I carefully laid my violin down in its case and showed her how there was a special place designed to hold the bow, and another space for the spare one I always carried. She spotted the packets of strings and asked what they were. I explained that I carried spares because of how easy it was for strings to break when I was playing, how strong and yet fragile they were. She crouched down while I tucked the bow away with real care. I explained that it's not just the violin which is valuable, a good bow is worth more money than most people think. She watched as I fastened it in place with Velcro straps, just like her wrist purse, and closed the case. Then I crouched down, hugging her to me with my left arm, the phone in my bowing hand. The girl wriggled to get her face nearer to mine, tilting her head and smiling. A practiced selfie-poser already! How old was she? Five? Six? Heads together, we smiled for the camera. I clicked a couple of shots and stood up. Immediately she reached for the cell phone.

'Show me, show me!'

I gave it to her and she skipped over to her mother. There were big smiles on both their faces now. They thanked me, bent their heads over the phone, and walked off. Just when I thought I was forgotten, Claire ran back and hugged my legs without a word.

Alone again, I told myself that I was done for the day. I had carried out the experiment, performed in a public street and, strictly speaking, lost my bet that no-one would notice me. But it wasn't all bad – I had been asked for an encore and even been presented with a bouquet of sorts, if you count that cup of coffee. I felt shaky. Performances, even rehearsals always drained me. Never mind my pride, it was time to go back to the hotel. I turned round to my violin case lying on the ground behind me, ready at last to go and make my peace with Mom. The space was empty. My violin was gone.

My first instinct? Call Mom. Who else? It had taken us years to find the right instrument for me. The one. The perfect match. She doesn't shout at first, in fact she doesn't say much at all. There's just this awful silence down the phone. Louder than yelling.

When she turns up, I've stopped crying and started shaking. Finally, I have my audience, there's a little crowd of people around me. Voices. Questions I can't make out, or answer. I stare at the empty space on the ground then my empty hands in frantic disbelief. I rub the hollow of my shoulder where my violin usually nestles. It feels naked. I made just one mistake. I neglected the habit of a lifetime: never to be separated from my precious violin, even for one second. It was my fault, I only had myself to blame, and yet I felt abandoned. Mind and body numb. Alone.

Mom's voice was the only thing I could hear. She was talking to a man who lived locally. She was asking where the police station was. We had to speak to the police. People were sympathetic. People were helpful. People were just plain curious. I wanted to get away, crawl into a dark corner somewhere. I had become a walking wound.

Mom took a firm grip on my arm. As we began to move, our way was blocked by the guy I had been talking to earlier. He had taken his sweatshirt off and I could see the tee shirt underneath. I focussed blindly on the words written across the front – JUST DO IT...

'Lost anything?' The words were fired at me.

I looked at him, too numb to speak. His face was a clenched fist of anger. Mom tugged at my arm and started to pull me past him. He put out his hand to stop us, then swung his rucksack down off his shoulder. I heard my mother gasp and felt her stiffen as he pulled out a bulky object sticking out of the top. It was wrapped in his sweatshirt and I felt it before I saw it. The case. My violin.

It took a while to persuade Mom to let the young guy go. The relief she felt had only made her more furious. I listened to a whole bunch of accusations. It was theft. I was a stupid fool. We must prosecute. He should get what's coming to him.

I didn't care. I didn't want to go to the police. I was in pieces and yet I was whole again. I had my life, my partner in music back once more. I didn't want to punish the young man so I bargained with my mother. She was right. She was always right. It was all my own fault for storming off by myself, for trying that stupid experiment in the first place. I promised I would perform at the reception and never question her decisions again if she would just let him go.

I knew her well enough to know this was the one argument that would work.

The young guy took no notice of her threats, didn't even acknowledge my speaking up on his behalf. He just walked away from the wreckage he had caused. Over his shoulder he lobbed,

'You should take better care of your fiddle. And your talent.' He stabbed a finger at me. 'You don't know how lucky you are!'

Back in the anonymous stillness of the hotel room I sat for a long time cradling my violin in my arms. I didn't touch the food or drink Mom ordered, I had the only thing I needed. When the phone on the desk rang, I took no notice.

The call was from the local newspaper. Someone, they wouldn't say who, had seen the crowd gather around me when I discovered my violin was gone, and had filmed the whole thing on their phone. The shock of the loss, the shock of the return. The witness had passed the footage on to the paper, a reporter had traced us to the hotel. Could we confirm what had happened? What was the value of the violin and was it damaged? Was it a Stradivarius? Had I needed medical treatment for the shock? Were the police informed? They said they would run the story with or without confirmation. They said they had stills of us all; me sobbing, Mom waving her arms around, the young man with my violin in his hands. We could hardly deny it. Mom wrote down a number on the pad by the phone then hung up. As she filled me in I knew what was coming.

'The publicity could be useful...'

'But, Mom, we promised him! We said we'd take no action...'

She shrugged and turned away.

'Please! He was jobless but he bought me a coffee – he was only trying to make me see sense!'

'You made me a promise too, remember?'

I shivered. She picked up the phone.

# The Blue Scarf

## Jackie Vickers

'She's welcome to stay here overnight. No need to go back to London, all that extra travelling.'

'But Marjorie's staying with her sister. All her things will be there.' Roy watched his mother finish the last potato, add it to the pan and start clearing away the peel.

'I still don't see…'

'Well that's what she's decided.' He went back into the living room and picked up the Oxford Times. His mother followed him and stood in the doorway, drying her hands on her apron.

'I wanted her to feel welcome, that's all.'

Roy turned the pages and said nothing. He thought his mother was most probably curious. She had spent ages peering at a group photo taken at the camp, complaining the uniform made them all look the same. He could hear his father moving about the hall. Roy put the paper down and went out.

'Back soon,' he said, putting his head round the door.

His mother sighed and went back into the kitchen. Roy and his father walked down the road towards the Masons Arms in companionable silence. They sat for a while savouring their drinks, wiping the froth from their lips.

'How long is it now?'

'Nearly six months. Apart from that one day-trip.'

His father grunted and took his pipe from his pocket and slowly began to fill it.

'Never easy,' he said, tamping down the tobacco with his thumb.

Roy nodded. It was true, he had felt apprehensive on first reading the letter.

'Still, the sooner you meet up, the sooner you can decide what to do next.' He struck a match and drew on his pipe, without much success. 'Most mothers wonder about the girls their sons take up with.' He paused while he had another go at lighting it. 'But you mustn't take anything your mother says too seriously.' He paused again. 'She's your girl, after all.'

But was she 'his girl', wondered Roy. They had had some fun during the war, but would they still like each other now?'

He had thought Marjorie the prettiest and the most lively of all the WAAFs on the camp. They had clicked straightaway, chiefly through a love of dancing. There were dances on the camp most Saturdays and sometimes in adjacent towns when time off and passes permitted. Marjorie was one of a group of shorthand-typists, working in a large typing pool. Roy repaired and serviced engines and was known as an ERK. Roy often wondered if his life would have been different if he had not been rejected for pilot training through poor sight. Despite the pep talks about how essential their jobs were, Roy still gazed up at departing aircraft and wished he were among them.

'Don't be daft!' Marjorie snapped. 'Think about how many don't get back.' She would be tapping her foot to the music, anxious to begin whirling around to the sounds of whatever big band was playing. Long shifts of aircraft maintenance, both before and after raids, alternated with slack periods of boredom, only relieved by frenetic activity on the dance floor. Sometimes there would be a couple of days leave he did not tell his parents about and they could escape to some London club, another boozy night and more dancing.

He had found it very difficult to come home, back to where he had been before the war started. He had got his old job back, as the company was keen to do the right thing by their ex-servicemen, though he now found bending over a drawing board from nine to five, plus most Saturday mornings, dull work. Furthermore, he had forgotten a lot in the intervening five years and felt insecure about every mark he made on paper.

'It'll soon come back,' the older draughtsmen said. 'You'll be off to night-school come September, and that'll help.'

There had been freedom in being away from home; new rules of course, but then a lot of the old ones no longer applied. He and Marjorie had had a lot of fun before he was posted to Italy and things got more dangerous on the airfields. Neither of them had been any good at writing letters, so at the end of the war, Roy had been delighted to find himself back in the same camp for a few weeks before Marjorie left. Demobilisation took longer for Roy and it soon became clear that it would take months for some, even years if you were unlucky or stuck somewhere like Burma. Still, at least you got a demob suit out of it.

'Fits where it touches,' his mother said, tugging at the sleeves. 'Still, we mustn't complain. Poor Mrs Wilson never got Peter back and Clive Burns, who lost a leg in Malta, just sits by the window all day. And don't get me started on rationing and shortages. You wouldn't think we won the war!'

Roy felt restless. Forgetting how often he had prayed for it to stop, all he could think about now was the sameness of his days. The first couple of weeks at home had been unexpectedly tiring and he spent a lot of time asleep.

His mother worried. 'He's too quiet, for a boy of his age. You'd think he'd want to celebrate, now it's all over.'

'Leave him be,' said his father, 'They got bombed a few times on the airfields. He's seen some bad things.'

'He can tell us. He can tell us anything, he knows he can.'

But Roy didn't want to talk to anyone, particularly those who wanted to hear about his experiences.

'You don't need to go easy on the gory bits,' one neighbour insisted. 'I was an ARP warden. I had to be ready for any eventuality,' he declared, stroking his moustache. Roy lay on his bed for hours and wondered how Marjorie had felt when she got home. He knew her family had been bombed out, but her letters were short on detail. She had said that all were safe, but it was difficult living with her aunt, who complained endlessly about small things, 'when we haven't even got a house left.'

Roy hoped Marjorie's visit might spice things up, she had always seen the funny side of everything. He tried to remember what they had said during their last night together. They had both drunk too much. Did they swear eternal love? Could they now pick up where they had left off? Always assuming she hadn't found consolation with that chap she was always looking at, Arthur from Grimsby, no distance from Hull once the Humber ferry was sailing again.

On Saturday he took his demob suit down from the peg behind his bedroom door. Like so many others, newly discharged from the forces, he had changed shape in the intervening years and was relieved to be sent home in something wearable.

'You might want to buy her something,' said his mother as he was setting out.

Roy was annoyed not to have thought of it first. 'There'll be plenty of choice in town.'

'Well don't waste time looking for stockings, like gold-dust these days.'

Roy closed the door behind him and rolled his eyes. Ideally, he would like to give Marjorie a big box of chocolates but rationing naturally put paid to that. He had been well-fed in the RAF, so ration books and the still half-empty shops took a bit of getting used to. He decided to go to Boswells, someone there might advise him. He had happy memories of their toy department when toys had been more plentiful than the money to buy them. He hung back until the pretty shop assistant with blonde hair and a bright smile was free. She confirmed his mother's remarks on stockings, they sold out within the hour. Gloves? But Roy had no idea what size. Nor did he know what Marjorie's taste was in anything other than martinis and dance music. Everyone had worn uniform all the time.

'We do have these,' and she pulled out a box containing two patterned silk scarves, one pink, the other blue. 'Nice quality, pre-war stock,' she said, holding the blue one up to her face. Roy saw that her eyes were the same colour.

'What colour eyes does your girlfriend have?'

'Brown, definitely brown.' Though he had no idea whether they were brown, blue or green. They had spent most of their time in smoky dance halls or dimly lit bars.

'Pink, then?' holding the pink scarf up to her face.

'No, sorry. I'll have to come back when I've made my mind up,' he said, feeling his ears redden and his confidence evaporate beneath the calm gaze of the shop assistant.

'Shall I put them aside?'

Roy shook his head and hurried out of the shop. In the end he went to meet Marjorie empty-handed. He paced up and down the platform. Was he early, or was the train late? His memories of small, vivacious Marjorie with the long dark hair had faded. All he could think of was the blue scarf highlighting those very blue eyes of the pretty shop assistant with a lovely smile. He didn't even know her name, though she made him think of an Eileen, or better still as an Irene. He would think of her as Irene.

Everyone back home tried to make the best of things, but as war-time post had been censored, the devastation came as a shock every time Marjorie came home on leave. Hull was only a few hours flight from German airfields and it had been assumed it would be an obvious target. But despite the ingenious construction of fake airfields complete with dummy aircraft and other useful devices, no-one could do anything to camouflage the river Humber, which shone silver in the moonlight and led enemy bombers straight to the docks and factories to the east of the city. Now that the rubble had been cleared away, damaged buildings shored up and window panes replaced, there were still large empty bomb-sites in most streets.

Her younger sister had nagged her to buy a ticket after seeing the dog-eared snap of Roy she kept with his letters. She had pounced on it.

'Which one is lover-boy then?' It was a group photo taken just outside one of the hangars.

He's the handsomest one there,' she squealed. 'Oh, Marj! Don't let that one get away. He's gorgeous!' Her sister had leaned over the banisters as she left. 'I'll have him if you don't want him!' she shouted.

Marjorie wasn't going to admit it to anyone, but she wondered if it had been a mistake to keep up with Roy. Perhaps they should have ended it when he was posted to Italy, or even when he had turned up again on the base. Or even last week, before she had bought this train ticket.

Though it was now early May, there was still a chill in the air as she walked to Paragon Station to catch the train for London, carrying a small bag and a packet of meat-paste sandwiches wrapped in greaseproof paper. Her elder sister, working there as a nurse, would spend a few days with her, then on Saturday she would take a day trip to Oxford to settle things one way or another.

The carriages were filling up fast and at this rate passengers would be standing in the corridor. Marjorie grabbed the last window seat before a young woman, wearing a dark green suit and a lot of make-up, could sit there.

'Visiting family? Or off to see the boyfriend?' And her neighbour launched into the details of her own journey without waiting for an answer.

'I've turned down more job offers than you've had hot dinners, but they wouldn't do. Being in the services spoils you, well it did me, working with officers you see, a better class of person. I've got an interview this afternoon, we'd better not have a breakdown.'

By Doncaster, Marjorie had started on her sandwiches. Her neighbour wrinkled her nose.

'I never eat meat paste, nor spam neither. I'll make do with tomatoes till we get some proper meat again.'

The train shook and rattled its way to London. Marjorie, having soon finished her meal, leant her cheek on the cool window-pane and closed her eyes, hoping her neighbour would run out of anecdotes and stop talking. There was a stale smell from years of accumulated dust and tobacco ash. Sweaty bodies had been crushed together on too few seats for too long. Luggage crammed onto the overhead racks made the netting sag. Even the train seemed tired, she thought, as its scruffy carriages swayed through stations which had not seen a coat of paint for years. Marjorie tried to think about Roy and what she had liked about him, but her memories were blurred. The early days of the war had been exciting: communal living, handsome young men in smart uniforms, Roy the best looking of the lot even though shy and uncertain. Then the bombing raids of the airfields started. Everyone knew about the terrible destruction of the cities, your city, your street, perhaps even your family.

The brakes shrieked as they pulled into Peterborough. Heavy doors slammed, platforms filled with passengers and luggage and porters. Why did she spend so much time thinking about the war, now that it was all over? Maybe she would feel better after next Saturday. Oxford was said to be a nice place, at least it would be a good day out. Marjorie pulled a magazine out of her bag, now the green-suited girl was smoking in the corridor.

As the train pulled in to Oxford station that Saturday, Marjorie saw that Roy was waiting on the platform. He looked quite different in civvies, with his hands in his pockets and wearing a grey trilby, which didn't suit him as well as his airforce-blue forage cap. He looked very solemn and came forward rather reluctantly, she thought.

'You've had your hair cut,' he said.

She slipped her arm in his and looked up at him. 'You look taller.'

They fell silent, neither knowing what to say. Then Roy asked her if she would like a cup of tea, but Marjorie was keen to walk so they left the station arm-in-arm, every bit like an old married couple. They crossed over the canal and went towards Beaumont Street, passing the imposing entrance to Worcester College. Roy knew it well as he had been taken into the grounds regularly during College vacations. Various family members worked there and, as a child, he had often thought that he, too, would like to work in such a peaceful place, but his mother poured cold water on the idea. She said there were lots of opportunities for draughtsmen at the Cowley works and he would enjoy working in an office. Roy wondered if he should mention some of the buildings they passed; he had never shown a visitor round. Marjorie seemed uninterested in her surroundings, which might be his fault, so he pointed out the Ashmolean Museum and the Randolph Hotel opposite but didn't know what to say, beyond naming them.

'That's the Martyrs' Memorial,' he said as they crossed St Giles towards a large monument surrounded by steps. 'It commemorates the martyrdom of some bishops in the seventeenth century.' He bent forward to read their names. 'They were burnt at the stake, over there, down Broad Street.'

Marjorie pulled a face. 'Isn't there anything more cheerful?'

'Well, King Charles stayed here during the Civil War. His court lived in Christ Church and his wife's court stayed in …'

She interrupted, 'I didn't know you liked history.'

'Difficult to avoid it here.'

'Well, Hull is proud of keeping the King out!' Marjorie was smiling now, 'We were all for the other side and locked the gates, so all the King's troops had to go back to Beverley. That was the start of the Civil War, or so they told us in school.'

Roy told Marjorie the names of the various colleges, stopping now and again to look through the railings. She said nothing until they turned into Radcliffe Square, as a weak sun began to filter through the clouds to illuminate the buildings.

'It doesn't seem real.' Marjorie looked around.

Roy was pleased. 'It is rather beautiful,' he agreed.

'Maybe,' she shrugged, 'what I meant was, why did no bombs fall here? There are no bomb-sites, no ruined buildings.' She waved around her, 'why is this place untouched?'

Roy shrugged. 'Some say Hitler wanted it for his headquarters after the war.'

Marjorie had hardly spared a glance for any of the college buildings they passed as they walked towards Magdalen Bridge, but she turned to look when a couple of students ran past, gowns flying in the breeze.

'Look, Fancy Dress.' Marjorie nudged Roy. 'Funny time of day for a party.'

'Those are students.'

'Do they always go about dressed up like that?'

'They have to. Probably get fined if they don't.'

'You know a lot about these colleges. Did you go to one?'

'Heavens, no! My uncle's a Bulldog. He tells me about them.'

She smirked. 'I hope his bark is worse than his bite!'

Roy stood still and looked at her.

'And is he chained up at night?' For the first time that day Marjorie shook with laughter.

'I see we're talking at cross-purposes,' he said stiffly, 'My uncle's a college policeman. They wear dark suits and bowlers. It's a sort of uniform.' He frowned at her, she was still laughing.

They stopped on the bridge and Roy pointed to Magdalen tower. 'Choristers sing at the top on May morning and everyone comes to listen. They say it's lovely.'

Marjorie took a packet of cigarettes from her pocket and opened it. 'Have you heard them?'

They leaned on the parapet and cupped their hands round their cigarettes to light them.

'No, I'm usually asleep. Six o'clock is a bit early for me. Afterwards people jump into this river.' He turned round and pointed down to the water, now slow and peaceful.

She started laughing again, 'And are they all wearing those gowns when they jump? I bet they billow out like black parachutes,' she was laughing loudly now.

'It's just a bit of fun, one day in the year. What's wrong with tradition?'

Marjorie tipped her ash over the parapet and a gust of wind blew it back in her face. 'I can't take any of this seriously. It's like a game, with some in black gowns, others in bowler hats and all the buildings like you get in old films. Nothing real.'

'Of course it's real.' Roy stubbed his cigarette out. 'What you say isn't real, well it's just part of ordinary life here. The colleges are big employers of cooks, gardeners, cleaners and so on. Most people have the same lives as in any other town or city.'

'I don't know how many other cities you know…'

Roy cut in, 'My mother's from Leeds, I went there a few years ago.'

'That's West Riding, might as well be another country. Anyway, nobody would jump into water in Hull, only little kids on a hot day. Look down at that river. Go on! What do you see?'

'Just ordinary water with pebbles in the bottom…'

'Exactly. Apart from the Humber and the Hull, both muddy, what we have are open drains. Hull is low-lying and you have to have drains all over the place, only they're open and mucky and smelly and there's no money for filling them in or covering them up and they're full of rubbish. Little kids fish for tiddlers in the summer. In the winter, when the fog gets bad, you have to watch you don't lose your way 'cos every year or two someone falls in and drowns. And never mind the stink from the Fish Dock when the wind blows across from the south-west.'

'I should think you'll be keen to get away if it's that bad,' said Roy, glancing sideways at her.

Marjorie put her cigarettes back in her bag. 'Let's look at some shops then.'

They stopped first for a cup of tea and some buns that were rather stale. Then they walked along High Street and Cornmarket. Roy hoped this would satisfy her, but the shops either sold the same goods as she could find at home or displayed expensive luxury items.

She wrinkled her nose. 'I thought seeing as you weren't bombed there'd be more shops. We've kept ours going in pre-fabs on the bomb-sites. All the large stores are there, except for Hammonds. It had a direct hit. That's just a huge hole in the ground now.'

'We've never gone in for big shops much,' he said doubtfully. 'There's Boswells though. My mother says they sell everything we need. Big isn't always better,' he added.

'It's a funny town, this. All schools and only one department store.'

Marjorie looked in the windows, giving a running commentary on the displays, but Roy was no longer listening. Then he realised Marjorie had turned to face him and was leaning on the window. She was talking to him.

'It's not going to work, is it? You've grown up in something like a fairy-story, all these posh buildings and weird traditions and the colleges being so important. It's not real life as I know it. Bomb-sites and drains and unemployment and no houses and no licenses for materials to build. That's the life I've come back to.'

'We were so set on forgetting the war, we never stopped to get to know each other,' Roy said with a sigh.

'We met slap bang in the middle of it. I don't suppose many people think straight. And what about those GI brides off to America? I'm off home in a few days. Just imagine being stuck in Texas or wherever!'

Roy had seen the shop assistant with the fair hair moving around in the window behind Marjorie. He wanted to wave but dare not.

A clock chimed four.

'I can catch the four fifty, if we hurry. Then you can get back to that shop girl you was making faces at.'

Roy reddened. 'I don't even know her name, he protested.

'Maybe not, but you soon will.'

Marjorie pulled the heavy carriage door shut and leaned out of the window.

'Keep in touch,' she said, not meaning it.

Roy nodded, 'I'm glad you came,' he said without conviction.

'Don't wait. I'd better grab a seat.'

Roy looked up at the station clock. He had time to get back to Boswells before they closed. He stepped back, waved, and walked briskly away.

Marjorie sank into a window seat and felt in her pocket for the packet of polos she had saved for the return journey. Her sister had suggested a night out dancing if she was not too tired after her day in Oxford. Marjorie was never too tired for dancing.

Irene was serving a customer, so Roy approached another assistant and bought the blue scarf. The last shoppers were leaving the store as he went to stand by the staff entrance, holding his brown paper parcel. He would not have to wait there long.

# Just Another Tuesday

## Andrew Bax

As Joyce waited for the bus there was nothing to warn her that this Tuesday would be any different from all the others. Off and on for over half a century, she and Florence had met for elevenses and always on a Tuesday. It was a routine that suited them both; apart from that and a shared interest in needlework, they had little in common. They had been friends at school and when they went their separate ways prim, beautiful Florence, groomed for marriage by her ambitious parents, was sent to finishing school. On her return she promptly fell for Lucien, an austere young man of lofty intellect who eventually became Wilsonian Professor of Byzantine Art at Pembroke College. Having neither the desire nor opportunity to leave Oxford, dumpy little Joyce had become a clerical assistant for the council and married into trade. He was a butcher and they lived above the shop in Walton Street. They continued to live there until his recent death, when Joyce was surprised to discover that she had become the owner of five houses and three race horses. Yesterday, one of them had come in at five to one at Pontefract, and she was bursting to tell Florence about it.

Florence, meanwhile, was waiting for the bus at Rose Hill. The walk from The Firs retirement home had made her stiff and she was wearied of its meagre comforts; still, it was all she could afford. It was alright for Joyce in her four-room apartment with a bus stop right outside. It was in that place in Abingdon Road with a live-in warden and an indoor swimming pool. When Joyce told her about that, Florence snapped 'I've never heard anything so ridiculous. Who wants to swim at our time of life?' But she mustn't get cross she reminded herself. Although it was a struggle to get into town, she looked forward to these Tuesday meetings; they broke up the week and Joyce was a good listener. And this week, she had something special to tell her.

Joyce was the first to get to Boswells, securing that table at the top of the stairs by the window. They liked it there because they could keep an eye on everyone else and see what was going on outside too. The staff were always friendly, and the manager usually came over to have a word or two. It was nice to be recognized as regulars.

Why hadn't Jimmy told her about the horses, she wondered. She knew he liked a little flutter – and why not? Her needs were modest, and they had never been short of money. She left all the money side of things to Jimmy. He was the business man after all and when he passed on – bless him – he left her very well provided for. So, when the trainer rang last week to suggest a little bet on Port Meadow, she had no hesitation in agreeing to £200. And she made a profit of £1000 – just like that!

Just then Florence emerged from the lift and weaved her way between the tables.

'You look happy,' she said on seeing Joyce's smiling welcome.

'I am. And I'll tell you why.'

As Florence listened to the Pontefract story she reflected on what she would do with £1000. It seemed a huge amount of money to her. She needed a new pair of shoes for a start. And it would be nice to go on a cruise. Somewhere exotic, like the Caribbean. Yes, the Caribbean would be really nice. And then what about the children – and the grandchildren and, goodness, the great grandchildren! Suddenly £1000 didn't seem a lot of money after all. What would Joyce do with it, she wondered. Probably give it to the first Big Issue seller she saw. Florence sighed.

'So I'm paying for elevenses today,' Joyce was saying. From the very beginning they had each paid their share because Florence always had something rather plain, like shortbread, but Joyce could never resist a rich and creamy cake, which cost more.

'Joyce,' she laughed, 'there's no need for that, but I'd like to celebrate your win with a little ...' she looked towards the display cabinet '... with a little carrot cake.' After a momentary protest she agreed to let Joyce pay.

'And I have some exciting news about Edwin' she said. Joyce settled herself for another long story about Florence's talented family. How it happened, she would never know. Five children: they came popping out as regular as clockwork until Florence looked quite exhausted, poor dear. And as for Lucien – you wouldn't think he had it in him! Thin as a stick and no conversation. Just shows you never know what goes on behind closed doors.

As Florence recounted Edwin's life history, one she had told many times before, Joyce tried to remember who he was. One of the younger grandsons, she concluded, the one whose parents weren't married. Florence had been terribly upset about them 'living in sin' until Edwin was born. Now they could do nothing wrong.

'And now' Florence announced, 'he's been offered a place at Brookes.'

'That's nice, dear' said Joyce 'What will he be doing there?'

'Cyber security' replied Florence. She hoped Joyce wouldn't ask her what that meant because she didn't know herself.

'That sounds awfully modern'

'It is. And Brookes has one of the best courses in the country. Hundreds of candidates apply, but they only take the best.' Florence knew she sounded smug but couldn't help it. 'And lots of good jobs afterwards' she added. Whatever it was, she was certain there were better prospects in cyber security than in Byzantine art. Sometimes she felt a little bitter about the hand that fate had dealt her. Lucien had been so wrapped up in his work, writing books that nobody read, and poking about in dirty old monasteries that he seemed to forget about her for weeks on end. But at least she had the family.

'Such a shame you didn't have children' she sighed, and not for the first time. And, as usual, Joyce replied 'But you've made up for both of us.' In fact, Joyce's only regret was that she and Jimmy didn't have children. He would have been a good dad, and with all the money he had been making, he would have given them a good start in life. Still, she smiled to herself, they had fun trying.

Theirs had been a marriage of harmonious contentment in which Joyce settled happily into a life of uneventful routine looking after Jimmy, and he always made sure she had everything she wanted. It was remarkable, really, how she had adapted to being alone. But in the dark, silent hours, Joyce was grieving deeply. All she really wanted was to join her Jimmy.

Now Florence was talking about Oliver. Was he the one in the BBC, or was that Rupert? Joyce tried to look interested, but a sort of sizzling sound made it difficult to concentrate. More of a bubbling than a sizzling she decided; she couldn't really hear what Florence was saying.

'... and do you know what? They said he couldn't come back unless ...'

Joyce suddenly felt very, very tired. The bubbling had turned into a kind of popping. She closed her eyes.

'... they had to agree to that, of course ...'

The pops were getting louder. And then there was no sound at all.

'Joyce! Joyce – are you alright?' No reply. 'Joyce!' Florence almost shouted.

She gave Joyce's leg a little kick under the table. No response. She kicked again, harder this time. Nothing.

Florence stared at her old friend, now leaning back in her chair with her eyes closed and her head at an odd angle. Never good in a crisis, and now shocked, frightened and confused, Florence scuttled down the stairs as fast as her arthritis would let her, and hurried home.

And Joyce went to join her Jimmy.

# A Life in Luggage

## Karen Gray

I can't really say why the case caught my eye. It was almost hidden from view in a cobwebby corner of a French flea market. I climbed over some framed prints, catching a whiff of distant garlic from the farmhouse kitchen dresser they were leaning against, and lifted the case from the stone-flagged floor. It wasn't big, just one handbreadth high, two handbreadths long and one and a half wide. Hand luggage size. The layer of grime that rubbed off when I ran my finger over its lid bore dusty witness to the length of time it had been abandoned in its lonely corner. I sneezed and rubbed harder, revealing more of the warm conker tones of the leather. A bit further and my fingers felt the tracery of initials darkly imprinted on the surface. E.V.F. – an intriguing clue as to who had owned this little travelling case. Whoever it was must have valued it enough to have their initials embossed on the lid. Or did they just want to be able to identify their own property at a glance? Was the owner a man or a woman? Did they travel on business or for pleasure?

I slid the stiff brass lock to one side. The catch sprang open with a click and I lifted the lid. Up rose the unmistakable, musty smell of leather and neglect. Inside, the unpretentious, dark green painted interior was cracked and peeling. Flakes of paint had collected at the bottom, making it look as though it had been well used. Had it been well loved? I decided that E.V.F. was a man, and a practical man at that. The sombre colour had a masculine feel and there were none of the silk linings and fancy trimmings that a lady on her travels might have expected.

On the inner rim of the lid I found the maker's name embossed in gold letters:

DREW & Co
Actual Makers
156 LEADENHALL ST
LONDON E.C.

'Actual makers'? This was an arresting, emphatic statement, as if the manufacturer anticipated some degree of doubt about their claim. Or perhaps it was a declaration of professional pride?

I shut the case again, dusting off the rest of the lid with a paper tissue from my pocket, revealing the marks of several dark rings branded into the surface of the leather. These were easily recognisable. The case had obviously served as a low table, but for goblets of wine, or mugs of Nescafe?

I started to daydream about how E.V.F. must have packed the case with everything necessary for his journey, carried it abroad, and somehow abandoned it, lost it, or had it stolen. Perhaps he even died abroad. How else would it have ended up in a Parisian market? And what happened to E.V.F. himself? I began to conjure up all sorts of explanations.

E.V.F.'s case, its worn leather handle snug in my own hand, went travelling once more; back to England where it still sits on the floor, but dust free and burnished in front of a low window in our spare room.

I could think of no way to find out about E.V.F. himself but I did manage to discover more about the case. Samuel Summers Drew founded Drew & Co, a firm making leather goods, in 1844. He also employed gold and silver workers. The firm was listed as Drew & Sons in 1903 and by 1914, the two sons, Ernest and John, had taken over. The same year they moved to premises in Regent Street, London, registered their own silver marks, and continued to trade well into the mid-1930s.

Knowing more about the origins of the case gave me an even stronger connection to it than I had felt at first sight. Discovering that Drew & Co had operated out of Leadenhall Street from 1888 to 1914 led to the conclusion that my case (it now felt definitely mine) must have been made in the 15-year period between 1888 and 1903, when the company name changed to recognise the sons. This made it a late Victorian, early Edwardian piece and giving me a tantalising glimpse if only a hazy one, of what E.V.F. – who was probably London-based – may have looked like.

Handling a vintage piece of luggage like this takes you back to the days when travel seemed far more romantic than it does today. Or is that a distant, rosy illusion? In the age of steam engines there were railway porters jostling to carry a lady's bags. No longer. You have to push your own trolley now. I have visions of people waving emotional farewells, or rushing to greet loved ones stepping down onto the steam-shrouded platform. But with the steam came smoke and grit and soot. Not quite so romantic.

The memory of finding my little travelling case came back to me recently when I read an old newspaper article about the history of Boswells department store in central Oxford. During the course of 2018, Boswells marked 280 years of service to the shoppers of Oxford, and it all started with luggage.

The story of Boswells and luggage stretches back to the reign of King George II when, in 1738, Francis Boswell, Trunk Maker, started selling 'travelling goods' at 50 Cornmarket in central Oxford. The Oxford Street and Trade Directories carried an advertisement in 1846 describing the range of goods on offer: 'Leather and Paper covered Travelling Trunks', (Boswells has ever been conscious of the need to cater for all depths of pocket), 'Solid Leather Portmanteaus', 'Carpet, Leather and Seal-skin Bags' as well as 'Valises and Hat Cases'.

It's one thing to read a list of the merchandise, it's another to be able to see and touch an original piece. During one of the many changes the Boswells building has been through over the years, staff members discovered on the premises an old leather trunk with the following manufacturer's label inside its lid:

F. BOSWELL

FOUR DOORS FROM THE STAR INN

CORNMARKET OXFORD

Such an evocative address for a business – so much more colourful than a postcode. I can only imagine the stories that trunk could bring to life. The places it had been, the owners who filled it with their precious belongings, the men who heaved it up onto the backs of carriages, or down stone jetty steps to boats in different harbours. Every knock, dent and scratch on that trunk tells a story. Objects do tell stories. Here are some of mine.

Luggage often accompanies the important milestones in life, like leaving home for the first time. Seeing me off to university, my father put me on a northbound train and found me a seat in one of the separate compartments off the corridor that ran the length of the carriage. A packed lunch for the journey went up on the overhead luggage net which was strung on metal brackets above the scratchy, plush bench seating. My brand new, carefully packed trunk with its sturdy wooden ribs was heaved into the luggage van, under the supervision of the guard. No chance of being driven up in the family car in those days. I worried all the way north about how I would get the trunk off the train, but the university had prepared for that and we were met at the station by a surprisingly eager gang of second year male students. My trunk and I got safely to the student hall of residence and I had already made my first friends. What if they were all young men? My father didn't need to know.

Owning your very own luggage has long been a symbol of maturity or coming of age. I can still remember the first piece given to me; a jade green, leather-look 'vanity case' as it was called then, tall, like a small hat box, with a handle on the top of the lid. The interior was lined with a silky grey printed fabric, fitted with pockets and frilled elasticated straps to hold a young lady's bottles, jars, potions and hairbrushes. This case was not made of leather, nor was it lined with real silk, as synthetic materials had begun to appear on the scene making items like this more affordable. There was a small mirror fixed to the inside of the lid which I could never work out how to use without holding the entire case up to my face. I had very few bottles or jars at the time, no potions and only one hairbrush, but how grown-up I felt carrying the case about. The problem was I had nowhere to go, so the case stayed in my bedroom, but I walked a bit taller knowing it was there. Some years later, I set off for the USA on what would these days be called a gap year. My parents expected me to take my vanity case with me. At last, they thought, it would be useful! Little did they know that I was intending to hitch-hike. Could I stand at the side of the highway, thumb out and green vanity case at my feet? I had outgrown it already.

When the time came to see my son off on his own gap year, I took him shopping for suitable luggage. Times had changed and we came home with a high-performance backpack, fitted out with separate compartments for different purposes, map pockets, hooks and straps to attach bed rolls and water bottles. It was water-resistant, rip-proof, lightweight and padded for comfort. I have a photograph of him, loaded up as he set off on his adventure, apprehensive but grinning for my sake. Me grinning for his. I've not looked at the photo for years but I could describe it in perfect detail, so clearly do I remember that milestone event in our family life.

Emotions often forge powerful memories. During a recent attic clearance I came across a relative's old suitcase and stopped short at the sight of it. In the 1950s, Barbara had left the family semi-detached in Leamington Spa as a single young woman and travelled alone to South Africa for a three-year working stay. She took this one, large suitcase with her; it was plain brown, made of a smooth and rigid synthetic material, with extra corner pieces riveted on for strength. She travelled both ways by ship, spending weeks at sea but stopping off at many exotic sounding destinations on the way. During these stopovers she collected several brightly coloured labels, symbols of the places she visited on the voyage. These labels were stuck all over the outside of her case. They became faded and torn, but she had never had any difficulty spotting her case when she arrived at her destination and had always refused to dispose of it. The brown suitcase lived under her bed, convenient storage for her South African souvenirs and I remember as a child going through them with her, feeling the weight of a flat, painted stone that showed a stripy zebra surrounded by dark stick figures with bows, arrows and spears. I thought it was a dance but Barbara said, no, look. The zebra has his head hanging down, the figures are hunters.

There were paintings on cloth, one showing a round hut with a conical roof and a single door in the wall, women in bright skirts and children herding animals in the foreground. I loved these pictures of a family life so different from my own but was less happy looking at the carved and polished black wooden masks, which I found rather scary. Barbara would hold one in front of her face and tease me, popping out from behind it and laughing. I don't remember laughing myself. For me, it was much more fun to swish the horsehair tails of the fly swats around the room by their beaded handles and pretend to make fire by rubbing two coloured sticks together while I listened to her stories about the 'natives' who had made them. It all seemed so far away but the souvenirs made the stories zing into life. We would pack the tales and the souvenirs away again, black masks at the bottom, until the next time, neither of us ever tiring of the game. Thanks to this emotional tug, the baggage of luggage, Barbara's suitcase has now found its place in my own attic, although many of the objects I remember have gone missing.

It is in the nature of progress that things change over time, suitcase design included. E.V.F. would have carried his leather case in his hand, as did Barbara with her stickered suitcase and I my vanity case. Eventually, someone attached wheels to one corner of a suitcase, and a handle at the other end so that you could drag your case along without having to bear all of the weight. This was one of those ideas that make you wonder why it had not been thought of before. It certainly made things a great deal easier, and I was never more aware of this than the time I took my elderly parents on holiday to France by Eurostar. I asked if they needed to borrow any suitcases and was told, no, of course they had suitcases. Only as I loaded the car before setting off did I realise that their cases were the old-fashioned type with no wheels. They were what my father proudly called lightweight – the soft top, canvas style with straps and zips to close them. Not heavy in themselves but when full, too much for my parents to carry, so I had no choice but to ferry the cases backwards and forwards between the station entrance and train platform, leaving a parent each end to 'mind the bags'. A repeat performance was given the other side of the Channel. When we finally got to the hotel and started to unpack, I found that my father had covered their belongings in each bag with a piece of custom-cut plywood 'to protect the contents'. It was their first and last trip on Eurostar.

These days, you won't find me travelling at all without my Samsonite 'Spinner'. This latest development means that I can walk briskly round the smoothly tiled acres of airports without having to bother with luggage trolleys or risk aching arms at the end of the day. The four mobile wheels, like castors, on the bottom of the upstanding suitcase allow me to propel a case, or even two, in any direction with just the lightest of pressure on the telescopic handle. Now that's progress. And modern materials mean that you no longer need the plywood. Never mind surface damage from coffee cups, you could almost take an axe to these cases, so strong are today's modern materials. But where's the romance? Something in me still prefers the lived-in comfort of worn leather, its familiar smell and feel. Give me a travelling companion that shows the passage of time and bears the evidence of stops along the way, just like Barbara's brown suitcase. Until I have to run for the plane, that is. My new case is very robust, very practical, and very efficient. But I'm not sure E.V.F. would approve of it.

Today's management team at Boswells, are well aware of the value and power of memory. As part of their 2018 Anniversary celebrations, both staff and customers were invited to contribute their recollections to a Comments Book. There are many fascinating recollections about 'good old Boswells'. One lady customer was moved to record an emotionally significant event in her own life; that of being taken to their luggage department in the 1970s to choose her 21st birthday present – a complete matching set of Antler luggage. Quite a prize in those days.

If the story of Boswells began with selling luggage in 1738, the ground floor luggage department is still known for its wide choice and good advice today. As well as serving local residents, I'm told that Boswells staff often find tourists coming in to buy an extra case because they have bought too many souvenirs during their stay in Oxford. Hopefully they were doing their shopping in Boswells, and no doubt they carry good memories home with them.

# Recovery

## Annie Winner

As Julie turned into the next aisle of the toy department, the large bag hanging from her shoulder sent a display of novelty balls flying. Mortified, she scrabbled around on the floor to retrieve them as they rolled energetically away. Another woman shopper squatted down to help and between them they managed to retrieve the escaped balls and load them back into their container, by which time a sales assistant had arrived.

'Thanks so much for helping,' Julie said. 'I feel such an idiot.'

'Don't worry,' the woman replied. 'We've all done it.'

'That's so kind of you,' said Julie. 'Can I buy you a cup of tea as a thank you?' She felt drawn to her rescuer's warm smile and the friendly interest in her eyes. She was wearing an elegant green jacket which matched them.

'Well, that would be very nice, but' looking at her watch, 'I have to be at the bus station in five minutes to meet my children. It was nothing, really.' And with a kindly wave, she shot off down the stairs.

Julie was in the shop to choose a present for her small nephew's birthday. She loved the toy department. For much of her married life it had been the best – and lately just about the only – toyshop in Oxford. It was full of memories of her children's lives; the cuddly toys, the Lego, the shelves crammed with everything a child could possibly wish for. Now they were grumping their way into adolescence and were too cool for old fashioned things like toys – screens were all they seemed interested in these days.

After she'd chosen and paid for the present, Julie went into the tea room and looked around for a free table. It was Saturday afternoon and the café was full. Julie didn't feel like having to exchange pleasantries with a total stranger, but there wasn't much choice if she was to get a seat at all. Ah! There was someone leaving a table in the corner so she made a swoop towards it, just seeing off a couple of middle aged women who had also been hovering.

While waiting to give her order, she tried not to feel tempted to get out her phone and pretend to the outside world that she had a million emails to answer and lots of games to play. So, she sat and looked pensively into the middle distance until the waitress came. As she waited for her Earl Grey and chocolate brownie to arrive, a flood of painful thoughts seeped into her mind and her eyes filled with tears. The weekends the children went to their father seemed to stretch out forever. She tried to take part in outings and trips with her friends to fill the gap, but with most of them she felt their paths were diverging. What she was experiencing as a single mother, soon to be divorced, bore little resemblance to their comfortable, even smug, existence in couples. She had tried joining things but it was difficult to get out in the evenings, and at the weekends when she did have the children she wanted to be with them.

It was nearly two years since Ted had left. Although she'd been conscious of a subtly increasing distance between them, she hadn't paid much attention to it. Life was a treadmill of work all day, the ever changing needs and demands of their children and having a bit of a social life. Then late one Sunday night Ted had announced out of the blue that he was moving in with a woman he had met in his running club. Julie had been knocked sideways into a silence so stifling she had been unable to find the words to respond. She just sat there staring at him for what seemed like a lifetime, white faced, her heart pounding with shock.

'You don't seem very upset,' he ventured. 'Perhaps you're glad to see the back of me.' She just continued staring at him.

Then a blinding flash of anger released her tongue from its inertia and some of the slights and resentments built up over the fifteen years of their marriage surfaced. Through tears of rage and hurt she struggled to grasp what had happened. She bombarded him with questions – how long had this affair been going on? Why had he stopped loving her? What about the children? How could he not have told her he wasn't happy – they could have talked about it, gone to counselling. Ted's responses were monosyllabic and he refused to discuss anything, leaving her all the more enraged and distraught. He'd made up his mind and there was nothing more to be said. She could have the children but he would want them to come to him every other weekend, every other Christmas and for a week in the school holidays. He packed a large suitcase that night, keeping out of her way. She went upstairs to spend a long and sleepless night in the marital bed. He slept on the sofa and in the morning he went to work and said he wouldn't be back until Friday night when he would come for the children at five o'clock. He would leave it to her to explain this to them.

As the waitress laid down her order on the table Julie was jolted back into the present with an aching throat and sniffed loudly. She swallowed hard and forcibly swung her mind back into drinking her tea and eating her brownie and getting home. As she waited for the bus to Kidlington, she felt despondent again, going back to that grey and empty house to spend Saturday night alone with the telly. Well, at least she had kept the house and to be fair to Ted, he had always paid the maintenance for the children. With that and her salary she managed pretty well.

The bus arrived and she climbed up to the upper deck. She liked the tree-top views of the Banbury Road, looking into the lush gardens and backlit uncurtained windows of early dusk in North Oxford. The children had always loved being upstairs on the bus too. Now they travelled more and more without her, and away from her.

She and Ted had to speak about arrangements and she was able to do that with some equanimity now. He was still living with his running paramour, as Julie thought of her. Her name was Petunia. A couple of months ago her daughter had let slip that Petunia the paramour was pregnant which caused a massive lurch in Julie's solar plexus. The news had set her back, the final blow to her firmly, but clearly not very effectively, suppressed hope of a reconciliation. How could he start another family at his age, and what about their children? How would they feel? She had been distraught for quite a while, reliving the anguish of those first months after he left. She tried to talk to the children about how they felt about their new sibling but their responses were gruff. She wondered whether Ted had told them not to discuss it with her.

As the months went by Julie got into the habit of going into town on a Saturday afternoon on the weekends she didn't have the children, doing a bit of shopping, often winding up in the Boswells tea room. One sunny afternoon she was looking through a book she had just bought in Waterstones when a voice said:

'Do you mind if we join you?' Julie looked up and recognised the woman in the green jacket who had helped her pick up the spilt novelty balls all those months ago and a man who presumably was her partner.

'Of course not. How nice to see you again.' The woman looked slightly puzzled for an instant, but then beamed as she recognised Julie.

'Of course, the lady of the escaped balls! I'm Tilly – this is Adam.' He was standing behind her, looking completely bemused.

'And I'm Julie. You spared me a great deal of mortification'. Tilly explained the circumstances in which they had met to Adam, and soon they were into an animated conversation about everything from the merits of Boswells and the impact of the new Westgate shopping centre on the city, to the latest national political news. The time shot by until Tilly looked at her watch and said:

'Oh my God! I've got to pick up the children from the bus and it will have arrived already'. She leapt to her feet, rummaged in her bag and dropped a card on the table.

'It's been such fun chatting. Let's not leave it another three months.

Give me a ring or email me and let's meet up another time. Come on Adam.' And they were gone.

Julie couldn't remember when she had so enjoyed someone's company so much. She hadn't ever found it easy to make friends, especially those she'd met as strangers like these two. She'd been charmed by the way they both seemed to share their thoughts so openly, by their knowledge and enthusiasm. She also appreciated them not having asked her any personal questions, although she had let slip that she was divorced. They seemed such a friendly and outgoing couple. On the bus on the way home she'd felt buoyant and cheered for the first time in years.

A couple of weeks later Julie sent Tilly an email suggesting they meet up again the following Saturday. Tilly replied straight away. 'Lovely idea but we're having a small party on Saturday to celebrate my 45th birthday– well not exactly celebrate – who would – but to mark it. Come! It's at 17 Victor Street. No presents, but bring some drink – about 8.00? Tilly'.

Julie shrank from the idea. She'd always found parties difficult, and the prospect of one where she wouldn't know anyone seemed daunting and her first response was to make an excuse and refuse. But her second thought was – why not! She could do with making some new friends, ones who hadn't known her as part of a couple. If they were like Tilly and Adam they might be compatible and fun.

As she waved goodbye to the children on Friday morning (Ted would pick them up from school and bring them back on Sunday night), she felt a lift in her spirits that she hadn't experienced for years. She would go shopping on Saturday morning and buy something to wear to the party.

Her nerve nearly failed her as she walked from the bus stop in her new dress. She'd chosen a vibrant colour which glowed against her darkish skin and black hair with its becoming dusting of grey. She stumbled occasionally on the uneven paving stones, being unaccustomed to wearing heels, not helped by the combination of terror and trembling anticipation. What was she doing going to a party given by almost total strangers where she would know no-one? But on the other hand there was the prospect of meeting new people who had no idea of her story. She walked up the path and rang the bell. She was half an hour late and could hear the convivial buzz from inside the house. To her great relief Tilly answered the door. At least she'd know one person – and she spotted Adam emerging from a doorway down the hall.

'Julie!' he exclaimed. 'I'm so pleased you could make it. Come on in and meet everyone. Let's get you a drink.' Julie found herself surrounded by friendly and curious party goers, all seeming pleased to meet someone new and full of questions. She felt warmed and valued by their interest. She'd been right to brave it and she responded with a charm and animation she hadn't known she could produce. She found herself in a small group debating the rights and wrongs of Brexit and surprised herself by jumping in to support Adam's views on the matter. The conversation moved on, more drink was consumed and the music was turned up for dancing.

'Come on Julie, let's dance'.

'Not sure I still can,' she said.

'Nonsense,' said Adam. 'It's like singing – people say they can't, but they don't even try so how do they know?'

As they jiggled around in the dark and crowded living room, Julie relaxed into the music aided by the couple of glasses of wine she had consumed. It was hard to continue the conversation in competition with the decibels of the music. When the tempo changed Adam gently pulled her towards him. Julie felt increasingly uncomfortable as his arms tightened around her shoulders – it didn't feel right being so close to someone else's partner. At the end of the song she broke free and asked him where the loo was.

When she came back down Adam had disappeared and she got chatting with a small group of people who were standing in the hall, laughing and arguing. She swallowed and drew a deep breath as she saw Adam emerging from the kitchen with a glass in each hand and joining the group, handing one to her. The talk continued. Julie was conscious of Adam glancing at her as he listened to the chat. Julie's pulse quickened, her breath shortened and she abruptly left the group and went in search of Tilly.

She ventured into a room off the kitchen which was full of snogging teenagers floating in a rather interesting haze of scented smoke, presumably the children of the house and their friends, but there was no sign of Tilly. She went upstairs again and was relieved to find her hostess sitting on the landing with a couple of other women.

'Ah Julie! Come and join us. We're talking about adultery.' Julie's heart missed a beat.

'Well I know how it feels to find you're being cheated on,' she said, angrily.

Tilly's face changed. 'Oh Julie, I'm so sorry, I didn't know. We've only just met,' she explained to her two friends. By this time Julie was further disinhibited by the third glass of wine and the whole sorry story came pouring out. Her audience was more than sympathetic, asked the right questions and about forty minutes later Julie felt like she'd lost five stone. The sympathetic ear of more-or-less total strangers, the wine and the emotional echoes from her encounter with Adam had unlocked something in her and she felt greatly relieved, shed a few tears and thanked Tilly and her friends for their forbearance.

'Don't be daft,' said Tilly. 'Come on, we'd better go back to the party.'

As she sat somewhat drunkenly in the back of the taxi that was taking her home, Julie reflected on the evening. On the plus side she'd met some interesting people and even exchanged a couple of email addresses, and the conversation about adultery had discharged much of what remained of years of rage and grief. On the other hand the person she had made the most connection with in the evening had been Adam and although nothing had happened, she knew it could. But it wouldn't. She couldn't do that to Tilly. They planned to meet up for tea in Boswells tea room in a couple of weeks.

Over the following fortnight Julie often found herself mulling over the party. She felt chuffed with herself for having had the bottle to go and actually meet new people, ones she had discovered she had things in common with. She had already heard from a couple of them and was meeting up with another single mother. Her children were about the same age as Julie's, and they had arranged to go for a walk the following weekend. On the other hand she regretted her outburst on the landing. It felt too soon to disclose such private stuff to people she hardly knew and it made her feel vulnerable and thwarted in the process of reinventing herself which her marriage breakdown had precipitated. She also thought about Adam. A lot. The warmth of his brown eyes, the scruffy jeans he favoured, the way he'd argued his case with passion and clarity. She'd liked the way he didn't interrupt other people and listened to their views even if he didn't agree with them. She'd liked the feel of his hands on her shoulders too.

The day arrived for the meet up they had arranged and as usual on her Saturday afternoons without the children Julie took the bus into town, did a bit of shopping and went into Boswells tea room for a cup of tea. Tilly had already arrived and was guarding a table for them.

'That was a lovely party,' Julie said. 'I was so nervous but everyone was so friendly and welcoming that I felt at home in no time. Just sorry I burdened you and your friends with my troubles. It must have been the drink talking. I'm not used to drinking that much.'

'Don't be daft,' said Tilly. 'Everyone thought you were great. Adam took quite a fancy to you! I said we'd be here this afternoon so he might join us later. He's taken the children to the cinema but they are old enough to get home on their own.'

Julie's heart sank and she felt herself blushing and her pulse quickened. She changed the subject, asking which of the youngsters she had glimpsed at the party had been Tilly's. They talked about their children and the challenges of dealing with the teenage years, finding lots of common ground and shared anxieties.

'We have the added dimension of two of the children being Adam's not mine.'

'Oh,' said Julie. 'So, you've both been married before?'

'Well, yes – of course,' said Tilly. 'Adam's wife ran off with someone else about the same time as my husband died three years ago, so it seemed sensible for us to pool our resources and share a house. We've always been very close and it works well. The problems will come when one of us meets someone else.' Julie was baffled and clearly looked it.

'But aren't you married to Adam?'

Tilly roared with laughter. 'No way! He's my brother!'

# The Dressing Case

## Jackie Vickers

Nora Armitage stands twisting the fringes of her scarf around her fingers. Thompson brought the car round some time ago and sits, his face expressionless, ready to leap out and open the car door as soon as Madam makes a move. Her daughter Daisy keeps them waiting most days, but Nora controls her impatience. In the run up to the wedding it is important that everybody should keep calm. A door slams and a tall, slender young woman crosses the hall, buttoning her gloves, heels clacking on the tiled floor.

'Are we off then?'

Nora purses her lips but says nothing. Thompson sees them settled and drives off smoothly. He likes these shopping trips to Oxford; he gets a full two hours there and back behind the wheel of the 4.5 litre Bentley. If the ladies stay to lunch he will get a further two hours sitting by the canal, watching the barges.

'I've made a list,' says Nora, rummaging in her handbag, 'we mustn't forget the hat-box. And Sylvia says grey is this season's colour ...' Nora's friend, Sylvia Stannard, has insisted that Boswells have all the luggage Daisy might need in their travel department.

'A complete waste of time going up to town,' she says, waving her cigarette holder around, 'Boswells has everything.'

Nora hangs on her every word. William Armitage had made a fortune from the war, (his brother called it profiteering) but Nora had felt increasingly uncertain in her new role as woman of means. Everything, from wearing the right shoes to ordering from menus, was a potential social pitfall. And Sylvia had guided her without ever patronising her. Nora would be forever grateful. Sylvia had even found Edwin for her.

'Just back from the Australian Outback, they say. Yes, really! Make sure Daisy grabs him before anyone else does. There's a lot of Greville land in Norfolk,' she said as ash fell from her cigarette, 'but it was entailed, so Hugh got the estates, years ago, when you still did. But the younger son, Edwin, got the investments.' Nora was impressed but tried not to show it.

'The Greville name counts for a lot, of course. Though the rumours are that they need the money,' she winked, 'you know, like the American heiresses coming over to marry our Lords and Marquises.' Nora sat down suddenly, making the chair creak.

Sylvia laughed. 'I'm not talking Blenheim here. On a much smaller scale, obviously, but still, landed gentry's son meets business tycoon's daughter!' Nora had to admit that a bronzed, muscular, outdoor type appealed as a prospective son-in-law.

Edwin, though, turns out to be a disappointment. The photo Sylvia has acquired shows a somewhat unprepossessing young man, with receding hair and very pale skin. Nora makes the best of it, but he has clearly not been ranching, or whatever one does in Australia. Nora doubts he was ever there. Can he even ride a horse?'

Despite her reservations, for money isn't everything to Nora, she allows Sylvia to fix an invitation to a weekend house-party, where Daisy and Edwin meet and discover they both feel like outsiders. Neither enjoys tennis and noisy parlour games, so they slip out of a side door and go for long walks; fortunately, their absence is not noticed. By Sunday tea-time everything that matters has been settled. Daisy is ecstatic but Nora still has her doubts. How does he earn his living?

William Armitage makes light of his wife's concerns. 'His family own half of Norfolk, what more do you want? Yes, I know he has no land but he's not short of a bob or two. Our Daisy'll be fine.'

Edwin has told Daisy he wants to be an artist. William will have other ideas, but the details can wait till after the wedding.

As the Bentley approaches Oxford, Nora begins to feel nervous about her ability to buy the right things. It is Sylvia who has found a dressmaker, advised on the dress, the trousseau, the bridesmaids, the flowers and Nora dare not ask for more help. Still, it's only a matter of a couple of trunks, some suitcases, a dressing case and a hat-box. Nora's lack of experience she keeps to herself. It need not be known that she and William had married quietly in a northern mill town no-one has heard of, then or now. William had inherited a very small textile enterprise, which was failing. Being astute, energetic and not afraid of hard work, he gradually built it up. He and Nora still lived modestly, employing only one servant for the 'rough work', ploughing everything back into the business. Then the war came. With the war came opportunities.

'They'll need a lot more men, soon,' William was ecstatic.

'What has that to do with cloth?'

'A bigger army, means more uniforms. They're not going into battle naked, are they?' He paced up and down, filling their small room with his bulk and his energy. 'Mind you,' he suddenly stood still, frowning. 'That's just the beginning.'

'You're not making much sense, William,' said Nora, bent over her mending.

'They say the Germans are re-arming faster than we are. So unless we get a move on they'll have more men with guns.'

Nora knew better than to interrupt him.

'So, there you are, more guns …bang, bang, dead soldiers everywhere. For every man you have, how many women, children, old folk?'

'Five or six,' ventured Nora. 'Perhaps more?'

'Exactly!' bellowed William. 'And what do families do? They mourn their dead. One way is to wear black. We can maybe compete for some contracts for khaki cloth, but what we really need, looking ahead, is black cloth and plenty of it.'

Looking back, Nora saw that this was the moment when William had foreseen a good deal. And it was this foresight that had laid the foundations of his now considerable fortune. As the years passed he bought a London House, then, leaving his northern factories in safe hands, he began looking for another house, this time in the country. Nothing too extravagant to begin with, but somewhere he could dip a toe into country pursuits. His war service had not been of the dangerous kind. His risks were all fiscal. With his own shoot, his own pheasants, he could at last enjoy his own 'bang bang' weekends, as he liked to call them.

As the years passed, Nora feared William would be ridiculed, for he was loud and clumsy, the tea-table was always at risk. As he grew more successful, he cultivated and even exaggerated his northernisms.

'I'm a Yorkshireman, and proud of it!' he would roar.
Nora would shrink in some corner, but the men laughed with him and the women seemed to admire him.

'Folk are much the same everywhere,' he told Nora. 'Don't think they talk behind your back, no-one really cares.'

But Nora knew this was not true.

Edwin Greville was the icing on the cake for them both. William could see the brass plate outside his London office: Armitage & Greville. Eventually Greville & Sons perhaps. Though he never thought to ask his future son-in-law if the idea appealed.


Thompson draws up outside Boswells. He leaps out and helps his passengers to alight. There is a restaurant on the top floor and Nora thinks she will be ready for lunch after the strain of choosing luggage.

'Three hours, please, Thompson.'

The chauffeur gives a little bow and drives away. As he turns the corner he is already singing as he sets off to lie by the canal, in the autumn sunshine.

In the leather goods department, Miss Stevens, grave and competent, attends to their wishes. She is old enough to be experienced but not out-of-date in her understanding of customers' problems. She explains what young ladies are 'going in for' these days and she counsels against too much hand luggage, for trunks can be sent ahead and unpacked by the maid.

Suitcases and trunks of all sizes are grouped by manufacturer. All the big names are there: Ebert, Alfred Gough, David Richenberg. Miss Stevens explains that while all suitcases are suitable for all excursions, longer trips generally require trunks. These have a strong framework and will take more bulk and weight. She shows them the most recent designs including the very popular dressing cases. Daisy catches her breath as Miss Stevens lifts the lid of one after another to reveal sumptuous silk linings, little glass bottles with silver tops, silver backed brushes and all manner of little luxuries, necessary to lady travellers. Miss Stevens assumes her customers are seasoned travellers, yet is careful to discuss the various options in a way that could not reveal their ignorance, should they never have travelled on a Pullman train or taken a berth in a transatlantic liner. Nora relaxes. William had taken them on one European trip, a few years before, 'to see foreign parts'. Having seen, he was satisfied and, to Nora's relief, did not suggest another. He did send Daisy to Switzerland to pick up some French, Art Appreciation, 'or anything else she fancies'.

William is magnanimous, even when he can't see the point of it. 'I expect you know best,' he says to Nora and Daisy, 'having been put up to it by that friend of yours'. But he says it with a smile.

Daisy has been captivated by the red silk lining, so they settle on the grey set of suitcases with dressing case. Miss Stevens goes to the glass fronted wooden cabinets to find a matching purse. That wasn't so difficult, thinks Nora, who will now be able to enjoy her well-earned lunch.

There are raised voices; something is happening by the stairs. Nora hears her name and William emerges from the crowd that are milling around. He is red-faced with beads of sweat on his forehead and clearly distressed.

'Don't buy anything,' he rushes up to her. 'Not a thing!' And he hustles a bewildered Nora out of Boswells and onto the busy street.

Miss Stevens, composed as ever, betrays no surprise and suggests to Daisy that she might put aside the luggage till further notice. But Daisy, excited by the many shapes and designs of travel goods, is reluctant to leave empty handed. She signs for, and takes the silk-lined dressing case.

Outside, William is pacing in front of St Mary Magdalene, away from the shoppers. He cannot understand why his expensive motor-car and matching chauffeur are not there when he needs them. He will call a cab and go looking, then remembers he must avoid unnecessary expense. Daisy arrives and says she knows where to find Thompson and hurries off before William can stop her.

Nora dare not ask William why they are rushing home, and Daisy, hugging her dressing case, seems oblivious of the tension in the back of the Bentley. The journey home seems interminable.

The stone-walled villages of Oxfordshire glow in the autumn sunshine; late roses and clematis flower in village gardens; the countryside has never looked more lovely. The Bentley's occupants see none of this.

On arrival, Daisy disappears and William goes into the drawing room and pours himself a whisky. He offers Nora sherry and asks her to sit down. He is sweating even more profusely. Then he tells her.

'I am ruined.'

Nora looks up at him. 'I don't understand.'

William's eyes are closed and his lips are pursed. He looks in great pain. Neither speaks for a while as Nora waits. And then William clears his throat.

'There's been a crash … the Stock Exchange … investments …' He cannot find the words to explain how or why he had invested so heavily in American markets. Not that he is the only Englishman to lose his wealth in the pursuit of rich pickings. The Wall Street Crash will be remembered as one of the defining moments in the nation's history.

William, a large and heavy man, seems suddenly diminished, physically. He pours himself more whisky and sits down by his wife. His legs no longer support him. Nora remembers those years before wealth bought them houses, servants and luxury cars. She walked everywhere, did her own cooking and laundry: a knuckle of ham was a treat.

'How bad is it?' she asks.

Meanwhile Daisy has had a visitor. A small blue Morris Tourer Convertible is parked some distance from the house. It is piled high with bags and boxes. An easel has been strapped on top. Edwin, always pale, now ashen with anxiety, suggests a walk through the wood. It is cool under the trees; Edwin shivers. They sit on a tree trunk.

'My family tell me I have probably lost a lot of money. There has been a crash in America which will affect people world-wide.'

Daisy waits.

'They think your father is probably ruined, that he will want to back out of our marriage ...' His hands tremble.

In the drawing room, William tells Nora that this house will have to be sold. They can manage if they live in the smaller London House with fewer servants and without the expense of the shoot. Thompson and the Bentley will have to go, we'll use cabs.' Nora listens carefully. A six-bedroom house in Chelsea, with four servants doesn't sound like ruin to her. And she will still have Sylvia for friendship and advice. Then she remembers Daisy.

William shrugs. 'She's young and a good-looking lass. Plenty more fish in the sea. Though he could always work! I didn't get all this,' he makes an expansive gesture, 'without a lot of graft.'

Nora is quiet. It seems to her that it is one thing to make money, another to keep it.

'Oh! But the wedding!' How could she forget all those months of planning and dresses already ordered? 'And what about Thompson? And cook and all the servants? And Millie?' Her maid Millie is the only one she can trust.

'Bring Millie to London, if you must. The rest'll have to shift for themselves. That's life.' Dog eats dog in William's life. He would still be living in Greasborough if he didn't understand that.

Daisy gazes at Edwin, not appreciating the gravity of his words. 'I am 21, she says, with a shrug. 'All my father can back out of is paying for the wedding! I think we can manage quite well without one of those. I'd been dreading it anyway. My ideal is to elope!' she says flinging her arms round him. Scenes from her happy childhood have flashed before her. Standing on a chair, helping her mother shell peas, her first attempts at rolling pastry, kneading dough. Too much to explain now to Edwin. 'We love each other,' she smiles, 'what more do we need?'

'This!' Edwin removes a large sheet from a white envelope. It is a special licence. 'I hoped you might … we might …'

'Elope!' she cries. Daisy, no longer dreamy and slow, jumps up. 'Meet me by the car in ten minutes.'

'Wait!' he calls. 'Have you ever been to Cornwall?'

She runs back to the house and up the elegant curved staircase to her bedroom. She scribbles a note to her parents, who are still inaccessible in the drawing room, and throws a pair of espadrilles, a bathing suit and various essentials into a large canvas holdall. She changes into slacks. She pauses at the door, puts her bag down and returns to pick up her new dressing case. She opens it, strokes the red silk lining, unscrews one of the silver tops, screws it back on, then closes the case firmly.

Edwin will paint and she will paddle. It is enough for now.

# Downsize

## Neil Hancox

Polly Arden spread butter on her toast and topped it off with marmalade. She looked at Henry, her husband of, how many years, fifty plus? He was oblivious to the world as he peered at the back page of the newspaper. She shifted her gaze to the garden, in particular the back lawn, the grass luxuriant but weed-studded, despite Henry's recent attempt to tame it. It was too much for him, four bedrooms were too much for her. Clothes, books, possessions were suffocating them.

She cleared her throat. 'Henry,' she said, 'it's time we downsized.'

He looked up from the crossword, across the rumpled tablecloth littered with breakfast debris, the healthy option of course, 'Um, yes my dear, what do you mean? There must be thousands of words beginning with the letter D, debt, disaster, death.' He took a sip of tea. 'There are cheerful ones as well,' he added, 'delicious,' he paused, 'but mainly they are unpleasant, draconian, damnation…'

'Stop it Henry.' She knew the signs, he was in puzzle solving mode. Better take the direct approach straight to the heart, well metaphorical heart. Her husband could be annoying but she had no desire to hasten his departure.

Henry continued to look at Polly expectantly. 'I repeat…'

'I mean my dear,' she said, controlling her annoyance, 'we need to downsize, declutter ourselves and our house and then consider moving to a smaller place.'

'Definitely,' he replied. 'Less detritus. Then I might be able to find things.' He smiled. 'Good idea.'

'We rattle around in here,' Polly continued, to emphasise her point.

Her husband demurred. 'We don't rattle my dear,' he said in a pedantic voice, 'because there is so much stuff we can barely move.'

Men! As she ate her last piece of toast, Polly began to feel deflated at the contrariness of her husband and the ease of her 'victory.' Had the man truly understood what she was saying? She had been planning the campaign for months, dropping hints, getting no response. Yet, as soon as the word was uttered there was agreement. What should she do now?

Further thought was forestalled by Henry. He finished his tea in one prolonged gulp, coughed violently, pushed his chair back and announced, 'The loft, that is where we should start.' To back his actions he disappeared upstairs into a spare bedroom and pulled the loft ladder to the floor. When Polly caught up with this activity he was balancing precariously on the final rung of the ladder with his body disappearing into dust and darkness.

'Found it,' he shouted as light flooded the storage space. 'The switch,' he added, 'and what a lot of stuff there is up here. Boxes, bags, an old water tank, deck chairs.'

Polly had intended to start the process with a skip, and by clearing the shed and carport. Today she had meant to float the idea and soften her husband up. But Henry had spiked her guns. 'All right,' Polly's voice broke into Henry's recital of the list of items, 'let's do this systematically.'

There was a crash and a yell of pain intermixed with muttered imprecations. Trousers covered in dust and cobwebs reappeared from the loft followed by a rucked shirt and bloodied head. Henry descended and stood alongside his wife.

'Don't drop blood everywhere,' Polly said, a little more tersely than intended. 'Scalp wounds always look worse than they are,' she added.

Her husband pushed back a wisp of hair, staining its whiteness with red. 'I caught my foot,' he explained, 'and then I pitched into those antlers. Where did they come from?'

Resisting the retort, 'a stag', Polly sat her man down, sponged his head with a clean handkerchief and reminded him about her father. 'He wasn't a hunter,' she said, 'but he liked collecting. Got that pair somewhere in the Highlands. Surely you remember, he brought them down here about thirty years ago and you refused to mount them on the lounge wall above the fireplace, said it looked pretentious.'

Henry thought deeply, winced, and remembered, an unpleasant interlude. It was a fact lodged way down in his mental archives and not easily recalled, though now he would not forget it, at least for a few months.

'How about a cup of coffee,' he suggested,' before my next assault. All workmen, or even work- persons,' he added with what Polly thought was a dash of insincere political correctness, 'have a tea break, even though I prefer coffee in the morning.'

They retired to the kitchen and he sat down at the kitchen table. A drink and biscuit appeared. Henry scanned his iPad, the emails were not interesting, the news depressing and the weather app agreed with what he could see through the window, which he supposed was reassuring. A large sticking plaster was eventually located by his wife in the medicine cabinet and applied to his head to complete the restoration of his equilibrium.

Having generated the momentum, however, Polly knew it would be a mistake to let it drop. 'If you feel alright,' she said, 'we will have another go, only with more care and less enthusiasm.' 'This time,' she said, 'I'll go up the ladder and you can stay below.'

Henry remained as instructed with a selection of black sacks and cardboard boxes ready to take trash and treasure respectively. An hour later he was still in position amidst heaps of clothes, pieces of carpet, a sword, children's memorabilia, moth-eaten soft toys, assorted pictures, a coal scuttle and a large aluminium cauldron, with the promise of more to follow.

Polly climbed down stiffly. Her left hip was really painful and her back ached from stooping. 'It's filthy up there,' she said, 'and I'll have to wash my hair again tonight.' She stood beside her husband. 'You haven't managed to bag much either to save or dump,' she observed.

Ignoring her comment, he pointed to the aluminium pan. 'I remember that,' he said. 'We used it to make jam, mulled wine and soup for our winter parties when the whole road came along, until you read about that scare that aluminium was supposed to soften your brain. That's when we banished it to the loft.'

Henry sneezed several times and returned to his wife's censure for his lack of success in disposing and sorting. 'It's difficult. You look at something and the memories often come flooding back. Then I get sentimental and indecisive.'

She didn't like to admit it, but Polly felt much the same, although no doubt about different things.

'Look at this,' Henry continued, unwrapping a large piece of green baize cloth, to reveal a selection of cutlery.

Polly examined the hoard. She screwed up her eyes, in lieu of glasses, to decipher the accompanying receipt. 'It was bought from Boswells,' she said, 'in 1931, by my grandmother I expect on one of her twice-yearly shopping forays into Oxford.'

The individual items were heavy, well balanced and silver.

'These are from pre-dishwasher days,' Polly said, 'when you had servants to wash and polish.' Henry agreed, 'too much trouble to use today.'

He hesitated before wrapping up the cutlery again and placed it with books and a copper coal scuttle in the heap designated 'Charity Shops, superior.' During this time each partner surreptitiously surveyed the other to ensure that there was no hidden backsliding.

Later, in the afternoon, after lunch and a thoughtful period which, in Henry's case disguised a quiet nap, the couple started to sort through the boxes of letters and photographs they had retrieved.

'How young we once looked,' Henry observed.

'Yes,' Polly replied, 'you had bushy hair and a trim waistline.'

'And your hair was black,' Henry retorted. He was not really in combative mood and refrained from further comment.

They made one pile of photos, 'for the children', though whether either of their offspring would appreciate the gifts was another matter. It was usually money, time and even patience that their families lacked.

Husband and wife agreed that it was sufficient unto the day and that a Chinese take-away, a bottle of wine and the offerings of the TV screen would see them through the evening.

'I don't think much of this wine,' Henry said quaffing another glass to make sure, 'and the TV programmes are puerile,' Polly added. Then they both nodded off before retiring for the night.

The next morning started as usual at the breakfast table only now there seemed less room and more stuff everywhere than before.

'It's a well-known phenomenon,' Henry told his wife, 'that half-way through any operation like this, things are much more chaotic than when you started, but if you persevere you get there.'

Rummaging in a cardboard box that had once held 24 cans of baked beans according to the label, Polly found a packet of letters tied with ribbon. While her husband was engaged searching through more photos and trying to match names to faces and places, she undid the ribbon and began to read. The letters were approaching sixty years old and from a very serious boyfriend. She almost gagged at some of the sentiment and at other times suppressed a sigh. What if she had said 'yes', where would she be now? In reality she knew probably divorced, certainly widowed. She had caught up with his progress through business and politics when, a couple of years previously, she had read his obituary in one of the broad-sheets. She smiled inwardly. He would have appreciated that sort of send-off, even if his success had been marred by several financial scandals and three divorces.

'What are you doing, Henry?' she asked as she broke out of the spell of what might have been.

'I've been thinking,' he replied. 'Maybe we will have less stuff but we should aim for better quality, so I have removed the Boswells cutlery from the charity pile. I think we should use it, every day,' he added with emphasis.

Slowly the couple were reclaiming their living space. Trips to the charity shops and the dump had encouraged Henry to sort through his library as he liked to call it. So many volumes unread for decades, and often unreadable when he tried afresh, had disappeared. 'Someone else might enjoy them,' he rationalised to Polly. She smiled in encouragement but doubted his judgement.

Returning later to the photographs, Henry had recognised one or two old girlfriends. Should he, should he not, reveal all to his wife? No, all families should have secrets, not too dramatic, but there was that adage about sleeping dogs and some of those people from yesteryear had a lot of common sense.

One picture Henry had retrieved from the attic was a different matter. He held it at arms' length and then propped it on a handy chair and stood back to admire it. 'This is from my grandmother's house,' he explained. 'It had pride of place in the front parlour.' Anxious to stop too much of his reminiscing, Polly removed accumulated dust and examined the scene. It was of a substantial size, an etching of two cavaliers, judging by their 17th century costume, duelling with swords in a large room, while several young women, in long lace trimmed gowns, and an alarmed looking dog, watched. Were the men serious, she wondered, fighting for the favour of one of the girls or merely putting on a display? She doubted if men three centuries ago were really any different from today's variety.

Polly sought for diplomatic words but could find none. She settled for 'Victoriana' and omitted 'hideous.'

Henry was disappointed. Perhaps it did look old fashioned, dated, and he now realised that the glass was cracked in one corner and the gilt frame was in need of serious repair. Reluctantly he put the picture to one side. He hoped it would find a good home.

Several days later Polly eyed her husband across the breakfast table, pen in hand and, she was sure, the cogs in his brain were whirring furiously. 'Saturday's prize crossword,' he said, in reply to her look. 'We might win this time.'

She shook her head. 'Henry, why don't you settle for a laurel crown as a reward for many creditable attempts. To win we have to complete the puzzle first.' She emphasised the 'we' in case her husband started to get delusions of excessive competence.

He nodded at the suggestion put down the pen and hesitated. 'The crossword puzzle is simply for distraction at the moment,' he said. 'I really like this old place and all the memories, and I've spotted a real bargain in the paper today, a special, high-power, battery-operated lawnmower designed for the active though older person, and if you order in seven days you get two bags of 'lawn weed and feed' free. With that I am sure I could tame our grass again.' He stopped for breath.

Polly took her time to reply though her mind was made up. 'I agree, now we have cleared out so much stuff, it's like being in a new house.'

Henry's eyes returned to the crossword. '20 across, 4, 4, "A loud engineer harmonizing with his surrounding environment – go away!" Feng Shui. Now that is really appropriate,' he exclaimed, 'a sign. Do you get it? I'll explain if you like.'

The missile, in reality a spent piece of toast, just missed his head. It was as well because Polly had been unable to locate any more sticking plasters.

# The Trouble with You

## Karen Gray

We don't usually go on a Wednesday. That's because I go to school now, and Mum is working. But today is different. Today is half-term and a special day.

When we get to Gramps's house, Mum goes in to get him and I stay in the car with Abi, as usual. 'I'll be two minutes,' she says. She always says that. It's never two minutes.

I wasn't sure about my little sister when she was born but I've got used to her now. She doesn't look like me. She's blonde and makes funny faces. Gramps says she's a real cutie, she ought to be on telly, advertising babies' nappies. She's good at pooey ones, Mum says. When we take her out, lots of people smile at her and ask what her name is. It's Abigail but we call her Abi for short. She looks cute but she's never still unless she's asleep. 'Old fidget bottom,' Gramps calls her. Mum says she's dreading the day Abi starts crawling.

While we wait for Mum and Gramps to come out I begin to count out loud, as usual. 1, 2, 3… Abi listens for a bit, then starts straining at the straps of her baby seat and kicks her legs. 10,11. I get one of the soft toys out of the bag Mum keeps in the car and wave it at her. She stops kicking and grabs it. I start counting again but she soon throws her toy down onto the floor of the car where I can't reach it because I'm still strapped in my seat. 17, 18... I hold out another one and Abi bashes it out of my hand. 20. Where's Mum? I wish she and Gramps would hurry up. By the time

I've counted to 31, the toy bag is empty and Abi is beginning to scream. She's not so cute when she screams.

At last, Mum follows Gramps out of his house. It's only as wide as one door and one window before the next house starts. On the window sill there's a droopy green plant. It used to have red flowers.

'Have you got your key, Dad?'

'Of course I've got my key!' He pats his coat pocket. 'You don't need to ask me every time! The trouble with you is you fuss too much.' Mum bangs the front door shut, comes to hold the car door open and waits while Gramps drops down onto the passenger seat, bottom first. He glares into the back of the car at Abi,

'What's all that noise about?'

She stops screaming and stares back at him. Gramps swings his right leg into the car, grunts, then lifts his left leg with both hands and heaves it in alongside the other one. Another grunt. Mum is watching.

'Alright, Dad?' He ignores her and she shuts the car door. She gets in on her side, starts the engine and asks, 'Boswells as usual? Or do you want to try somewhere different today as it's your birthday?'

'Why would I want to do that? Bloody silly idea.'

After we've parked the car with Gramps's special sticker and gone into the shop we find a lady with a purpley-blue scarf and a shopping trolley waiting for the lift. She says she's not in a hurry and lets us go ahead of her. Even Gramps says thank you. He gets in the lift with Abi in the buggy, as usual, taking up all the room because the lift isn't very big. Mum and I go up the stairs, as quick as we can, and meet them outside the lift on the next floor up. We go round the corner into the café, find an empty table and a highchair, then Mum settles us at the table and sits down herself. 'This do you, Dad?' He takes his coat off, puts it on the back of a chair and looks across at the table by the window where a man and a woman are sitting with a pot of tea. That's his favourite table. Mum is watching him. Before he can say anything, she passes him the menu. 'Here you are, Dad, what do you fancy? You can have anything you like today, birthday treat!' Gramps is still staring at the menu when the waitress comes over and asks if we're ready to order. We all sit quiet, even Abi, while he runs his knobbly finger slowly down the page. Mum orders two coffees, a quiche and salad for herself, a portion of chips and, as it's a special day, some apple juice for me and Abi with a glass of water to dilute it. Mum says juice isn't good for our teeth. We wait a bit longer. The waitress looks around at the other tables, clicks the end of her pen, it's a bright blue pen, and asks Gramps if he's decided what he would like.

'Don't rush me...' He scratches his head then says, 'Baked potato, beans and cheese. Plenty of cheese mind!'

I can't stop myself. 'But you always have that, Gramps!'

'That's because I know what I like. You always have chips, don't you?'

I hear chairs scraping as the people sitting at the table by the window get up and leave. Gramps sees them go and pushes his own chair back but before he can get up, the lady with the purpley scarf, who let us go up before her in the lift, walks over. She parks her shopping trolley at the table by the window and sits down facing us. Mum waves at her, Gramps makes a cross face. Abi starts to fidget in her high chair, reaching for things on the table. I'm just about to start counting out loud to her when the waitress brings the drinks. Mum gets some rice cakes and a jar out of her great big shoulder bag to feed Abi. She's always got everything in that bag. Gramps is still staring his grumpy stare at the lady by the window. She doesn't notice because she's busy piling up the cups and saucers left on the table. The waitress brings our food and asks if we want any sauces. She goes off to get me some tomato ketchup. Then it starts.

Gramps picks up the pepper pot. Mum looks at me. Gramps shakes the pepper on the table, peers at it, then shakes some more on his baked potato. He puts the pepper down by his plate and picks up his knife and fork.

'Do you want a paper serviette, Dad?' Mum offers him one and when he takes it, moves the pepper pot away. She can be quite sneaky. She plays these tricks on Abi sometimes.

'What do I need this for? The trouble with you is…' Mum shakes her head at him. Gramps forks a mouthful of beans into his mouth. It's piled up with grated cheese and some falls off onto the table. It's the orangey sort he likes best. When Mum starts to spoon something gooey into Abi, Gramps reaches for the pepper. Mum and I look at each other. He shakes pepper all over his potato again, puts the pot down but keeps his hand on it.

'Dad, I think you've got enough on there.' She takes the pepper pot from him and puts it in the middle of the table. Gramps grabs it back and bangs it down on his side of the table. Mum doesn't look at me this time. Abi squawks for more goo, Gramps turns to me and winks. We all have some more food, except for Mum. She's still busy with Abi. Gramps looks down at his plate.

'They never put enough cheese on these potatoes…'

Mum takes no notice, but I think she's pretending. Gramps reaches to pick up the pepper again but this time Mum gets there first. She was pretending! Then she grins, holding up the pepper pot in one hand, gooey spoon in the other.

'Yes!'

My Mum does funny things sometimes, but the lady by the window looks up from her coffee and smiles. I think she's been watching us.

I've eaten all my chips by the time Gramps is only halfway through his potato. Mum sniffs at Abi, makes a face and then gets up saying she's going to take her up to the toilets for a nappy change. We nod. As usual. Gramps watches her as she heads for the stairs then pulls something out of his trouser pocket.

'Here. You know it's my birthday today?' I nod again. 'Well there's something I want you to do for me, lad. Take this and buy yourself a present.' He puts some money down on the table. 'You know where the toy department is?'

'Yes, just over there, but…'

'No buts!

'…Mummy doesn't let me…' Before I can tell him I'm not allowed to go off by myself, Gramps carries on.

'The trouble with you youngsters is you've got no sense of adventure. You're mollycoddled, that's what you are. All this being driven around in cars…' He prods my chest with his finger. The knobbly one he shakes at you when he's cross. 'When I was a boy my mother used to bring me here on the bus, regular like. She'd let me loose in the toy department sometimes. I remember there was a working train set, I used to watch it go round and round for ages.' Gramps sighs and pushes the money across the table. I feel a bit funny. What would Mum say? Gramps carries on, 'We only ever bought something if it was Christmas or my birthday, just like today. And just like on your mother's birthday.' He grins at me. 'I used to bring your Mum here when she was a little girl, although come to think of it, in those days, the toy department was in the basement, you had to go down these big wooden stairs with bannisters…' Gramps goes quiet for a bit and I think he's forgotten about the money, but then he gives me another prod. 'Go on, the Lego's just over there. I'll watch out for you and tell your Mum where you've gone when she gets back.'

'But Gramps, Mum wouldn't like it.' I feel worry tears welling up inside me. Gramps looks at me, then his face goes all droopy, not a bit like his cross face where his eyebrows squash up together.

'Alright, alright, don't fret. I just wanted you to have a bit of an adventure, do something all by yourself, like a proper boy.' He pats my arm. 'There, there, lad, it doesn't matter.' But he doesn't look very happy.

Then I remember something I've always wanted to do. I get off my chair and Gramps looks up from his potato.

'What's up?'

I can see the lady with the shopping trolley looking at me.

When that little boy went off by himself after the mother had gone upstairs, I must admit, it did seem odd, in fact it worried me a bit. Where was he off to like that and why did the old chap let him go? In fact, I saw the boy hesitate and turn round, but his grandad, I assumed it was his grandad, waved him on. Quite brusquely I thought. I don't usually watch other people in the Tea Room, there's nothing worse than a busybody poking their nose into other people's business, but after I'd let the old man and the baby in the buggy use the lift ahead of me, I went up to the Ladies on the second floor, came back down to the first, and there they were again, in the Tea Room. By the time I had parked my shopping trolley next to the window, sat down facing the room (I do like a view) and ordered my bowl of soup, they seemed to be playing some sort of game with the condiments to amuse the children. It looked a bit like that old game of shove ha'penny from where I was sitting. The mother won.

Anyway, the boy trotted off in the direction of the Lego display and I think the old man must have nodded off, because when the boy disappeared round the corner to where the lift was, the old man didn't move. The Tea Room was quite full, it being lunchtime, but most people were busy chatting or eating. I think I was the only one who saw him go. I thought it best to sit and wait until the mother came back, just in case. To say that she wasn't best pleased to find the boy gone off alone is an understatement. Things got quite heated. The grandad raised his voice, wagged his finger, and the baby began to cry. The boy's mother, with the baby still in her arms, found the waitress who had taken their order and the pair of them went back upstairs. That's where you go for the lost property office. They had my scarf when I dropped it here once. So that left the old man and the buggy at the table. 'And then there was one…' as they say. He sat still for a bit, but the next thing I knew, he'd got up and walked off in the direction the boy had gone, a bit stiffly I thought. Probably his hip. He left his coat on the chair too. My soup had arrived while all this was going on. As I took a few sips,

I wondered if I should keep an eye on the buggy and the coat. As it turned out it's a good job I did.

My Gramps knows how much I love Lego, I've got a big plastic box of it at home but I have to keep it away from Abi because the bits are so small. Usually there's no time to stop and look at all the toys when we come to Boswells. Mum says we have to get Gramps home and Abi back for her afternoon sleep. We always go straight to the lift by the Lego. There are two Lego spacemen on the lift doors. The one at the top is a robot and is floating upside down. I think he must actually be in space. The bottom spaceman is holding something green, maybe an oil can for the spaceship, and he's grinning. Mum lets me push the button for the lift to come and take Gramps and Abi back downstairs. The doors are bright yellow, just like Mum's sunflowers in our back garden, and there's a shiny red stripe on the wall all round the edge. LIFT is written at the top with big letters in different colours. Lego colours. I can read them now I am in year 1 but I can't go through those yellow doors because I have to go down the stairs with Mum. She says it's enough for Gramps to manage Abi on his own.

So that's what I'll do to make Gramps happy. I'll go through the yellow doors into the lift. Then I'll go down, get out, get back in again and come back up. Maybe I'll get back to Gramps before Mum does. That's a proper adventure and Gramps will be proud of me.

I go to the lift and push the button with the down arrow. The yellow doors open and I go inside and push the bottom button. I feel as if I want to come straight out again but it's too late, the doors close. There's not much to see inside the lift, it's not a bit like a spaceship. No windows. It's not long before the lift stops and the doors open. I get out and a man carrying an ironing board gets in. The doors close. I don't know what to do. If I go straight back up, there won't be much to tell Gramps. I look around me and suddenly, I get my wobble feeling. I'm not where I want to be. I'm not by the birthday cards. Where are the books round the corner by the stairs where Mum and I usually go up and down? Where are the doors to the street? The worry tears are coming back again. I want Mum. Where has the Lego lift brought me?

Well, while the boy and his grandad were away, watching that buggy kept me occupied for quite a while. Another waitress came along to clear their table but she saw the coat and the buggy, and went away again. One man tried to sit down at the table, but I soon told him it was taken. My soup had gone cold by now. Eventually the mother and baby came back. When she saw that the grandfather had disappeared, her face was a picture. She looked around her and didn't seem to know what to do. Good luck to you finding either of them here, I thought. This store is like a maze. Two different staircases, five separate doors out onto the street, and then there's the lift. You could look all day and never see them. And if the child went outside… Well, it was as plain as the nose on anyone's face how worried she was. When I saw her struggling to get something out of her bulging shoulder bag with one hand, while balancing the wriggling baby in her other arm, I decided it was time to get involved.

Outside the lift is scary. I don't know where I am and I don't know what to do. I look for the doors where we go out onto the street. From there, I know the way to the stairs, I'll go up them as usual, and be back in the café with Gramps. I go round and round but I can't find the doors to the street. There aren't any doors to the outside, or any windows. I can't see the counter, the one with all the chocolates that we go past on the way to the stairs. Where is it? I must be in the wrong shop. How can I get back to the right one? I feel a pain in my tummy. I wish I was back with Mum and Abi.

I stand still for a minute and then I remember what Mum says. She always tells me, if I get lost, I have to find a granny-lady. I must tell her Mum's mobile number and ask her to ring it. Mum taught me how to sing her number, we used to practice it a lot. Mum sang her number to a tune, like a nursery rhyme, while I clapped in time, then I sang it and she clapped. She got the idea from the song you sing to learn the alphabet but we haven't done it much since Abi was born. I sing the phone number song in my head now and my tummy feels a bit better.

By the time I'd introduced myself to the mother and we'd settled the baby in the buggy, the grandfather – I was right about that – came back. His daughter was more cross than relieved to see him when she heard what had happened, but he took no notice and told us he'd remembered that the toy department was spread over three separate rooms and he thought the boy might have got lost. He'd been into all of them, the Lego section, the games room, the party shop, everywhere, but the little boy was nowhere to be seen. I joined in to say that if the boy had gone upstairs, his mother would have seen him. Maybe he had gone down the stairs, or in the lift?

'Who are you?' said the old man.

Well, I was so surprised I didn't know what to say. The mother put her hand on his arm, 'This lady's trying to help, Dad, but no, he never goes in the lift alone, does he.' She looked at her father for confirmation. He opened his mouth as if to agree, then he seemed to think of something and shut it again. A waitress came over to say that we should stay in the Tea Room in case the little boy came back. The staff had put out the word to look for him and they were watching every one of the five doors to the street. She asked if we would like some more coffee while we waited. I asked if I could have tea. I sat down, then remembered my shopping trolley and got up to go and fetch it. As I wheeled it back across to the mother she was rocking the buggy backwards and forwards with one hand trying to get the baby to sleep and looking at the phone in her other hand.

'Where's your father gone now?' I asked.

I'm just telling the nice lady in the dark blue uniform that I'm in the wrong shop and can she please help me phone my Mum, when I feel a hand on my shoulder. It's Gramps! He explains who he is to the lady. I feel all happy again, the lady says she is very happy and I think Gramps is happy but he doesn't say so. The shop lady gets me to sing Mum's phone number to her and then rings her straight away. We say thank you to the lady and Gramps holds my hand and takes me over to the lift past a lot of saucepans. I ask him will Mum be very cross with me and how are we going to get back to the café. Gramps explains that all we have to do is go up in the lift again, but up two floors as we were down in the basement, I'd come too far. I squeeze his hand because I feel a bit shaky. Gramps squeezes my hand back. When we get to the lift he doesn't press the button, instead he says not to worry about Mum, because he's got an idea, but we have to have a little chat about it first.

After we have the chat, I go in the lift and Gramps stays outside just as he said. I push the button Gramps showed me. I don't really like it when the doors close and shut me in on my own but just like Gramps said, when the doors open again, there I am, back in the right shop, and I can see all the Lego. It's like magic. And there's Mum, sitting at our table with Abi asleep in the buggy. The lady with the shopping trolley is talking to her. When Mum sees me, she jumps up and she looks like she's going to cry. She hugs me so tight I'm squashed. She asks me where I've been and am I alright and why did I go and what did I think I was doing, but before I can say anything, Gramps appears. He says hello to me and what's all the fuss about to Mum, but nothing to the lady. Then he sits down. There's quite a bit of talking after that. Mum says she didn't know I could work the lift. She says she's glad I had a go in it at last, but I mustn't do it again on my own. She says she's proud of me for finding my way back by myself and the lady says yes, well done and pats me on the head. Mum's not really cross at all, she looks pleased, a bit tired maybe, but definitely pleased. Gramps winks at me. Mum sees the wink. When the lady with the trolley hears about my phone number song, she says what a good idea and if she had grandchildren she would teach them her number. Mum suddenly asks did I really find my way back all by myself?

Gramps says yes, of course, but I know that's not right so I tell her no, Gramps found me and showed me how to come back up in the lift.

'Aaah, I see!' says Mum looking at Gramps. He grunts, fidgets on his chair like Abi and wags his finger at me, 'The trouble with you, my lad, is you're too clever by half.'

I'm worried he's cross.

But Gramps is smiling.

# A Job with Prospects

## Andrew Bax

There was a time, not many years ago, when that distant, dusty city seemed to shake off the shackles of centuries. People had money; they laughed, went to the cinema. Even the occasional bomb failed to staunch the upsurge in relief and optimism. But as the bombers became bolder the young and able began to leave; at first it was a trickle but quite quickly it became a flood. Soon that distant, dusty city began to collapse upon itself and there was no more laughing. As it had so many times in the past, it awaited its fate with resignation.

Among those left waiting was a good doctor. Everyone called him the good doctor; he was almost the only one left. When he ordered his son to leave the city, he stayed; when he ordered his daughter to leave, he stayed. Day and night he did what he could to save the sick and maimed. Even when his wife was paralysed by a bomb, he carried on working. She was a teacher and 23 of her pupils died that day but the world, wearied of such stories from that distant, dusty city shrugged its indifference.

Hamid didn't know about that bombing. He thought his mother had had a stroke. He knew things were bad back home but the intermittent power supply allowed only fleeting communication. So his father didn't know how bad things were in Oxford. Two years ago a grateful patient had lubricated the system so that his arrival was quick, comfortable and legal. The plan was for him to complete his medical education and join his father's clinic which, God knows, was always in such desperate need. At Oxford they didn't recognise the qualifications that he had gained in that distant, dusty city and, in any case, the costs were far beyond his reach. Unknown to his father, Hamid had become a taxi-driver.

After a while there was a lull in the bombings. There were rumours of negotiations. Units of the army, there to defend the city, began to drift away; some joined the wild men in the mountains, taking their weapons with them. The city held its breath, awaiting the next catastrophe.

The good doctor took advantage of the lull to send his daughter to Sydney, where his brother was in business. Ayesha had to be smuggled out of the city, her parents beside themselves with worry. Hamid was strong, resourceful and, after all, a man. Ayesha was young and innocent and had a sheltered upbringing. Even in crowds, particularly in crowds, her all-enshrouding burqa was little protection. Any unaccompanied young woman was at risk and they knew she would be groped, propositioned and humiliated. All of these things happened, but nothing worse.

Ayesha was mesmerised by Australia; by its light and brightness, and by its atmosphere of affluence and happiness. She was fascinated by the sea, which she had never seen before. Everyone seemed relaxed; there was no fear and tension and, above all, no bombings. There was running water and electricity all the time, and all the buildings were air-conditioned. And the colour! Back home the buildings, the roads and the mountains that surrounded that distant, dusty city were the colour of dried mud. Dust from that mud covered everything and filled the air too, so the sky was never the same clear blue as in Sydney.

She shared her exhilaration with Hamid, who phoned her every day. He told her that when he first arrived in Oxford he, too, was struck by so much colour. Only the old university buildings, he told her, were the colour of that distant, dusty city. While never quite admitting that he had abandoned a medical career he told her that he was saving up to pay for his tuition fees. The best money, he discovered, was to be earned outside normal working hours. So he was driving taxis into the early hours and doing quite well. During the day he took lessons in business studies, and slept.

Almost as soon as she arrived Ayesha had applied to study accountancy at the local college. In the meantime she worked in her uncle's office. Although determined to assimilate with her adopted homeland, she struggled to abandon her hijab. It was a symbolic reminder of the distant, dusty city where her parents still lived and she felt exposed without its protective folds of fabric. Of course, she couldn't wait to be rid of her stifling, stuffy burqa but she always dressed demurely and never went out without covering her head.

Hamid teased her about that, but he understood how she felt. Out of respect for their parents he sometimes attended Friday prayers at the Stanley Road mosque. But in other respects, he looked forward, never back. He had decided to go into business like his uncle in Sydney and, despite giving up on medicine, he was determined to make his parents proud of him. Ayesha called him a dreamer.

Hamid rented a house in Littlemore with six others, all of them immigrants from around the world. All of them had hopes and dreams of a better life than the one they left behind and all were in occupations shunned long ago by Britons. Through one of them, Hamid was introduced to D.F. Williams Cleaning Services. Starting at 2.00am and continuing for the next seven hours, he joined a team cleaning offices on the outskirts of town. So now he had two jobs which nearly doubled his earnings. Though exhausted, Hamid felt he was making progress.

Ayesha was making progress of a different kind in Sydney. Her hijab marked her out as different, and she didn't like that. She wanted to look like everyone else. So, one day, feeling guilty but determined, she stepped out wearing jeans and T-shirt and with her head uncovered. For the first time in her life she felt the breeze in her hair; strangers smiled at her; she felt alive and liberated. For the first time in her life Ayesha began to realise that she was beautiful.

Then, although the world's attention had moved elsewhere, that distant, dusty city featured briefly as a footnote in the news. And the news was not good. Hamid and Ayesha made frantic attempts to contact their father, efforts that were frustrated by the erratic power supply so necessary to keep his phone charged. Although they didn't believe him, he did his best to assure them that all was well.

But, of course, all was not well. The wild men had swept down from the mountains and were patrolling the streets in pick-up trucks loaded with gunmen who shot in the air, at passing traffic or at anything else that claimed their attention. The city's leaders were lined up and shot to discourage further such presumption. And for the next weeks and months, others who offended the wild men's creed were hunted down and dealt with. The good doctor knew he was on their list. His family name betrayed an ancestral allegiance to the wrong sect but worse, for worse – he had been treating women unchaperoned by their husband or guardian. Sometimes, even without their knowledge.

There was nothing for him to do. His clinic had been ransacked and closed; a few brave, desperate patients visited him furtively in his flat. The wild men were on guard everywhere and there was no escape. So, like everyone else, he kept off the streets, prayed and waited.

Hamid wasn't waiting. His manager at D.F. Williams had transferred him to one of the city-centre teams; more offices, some university libraries and laboratories – and Boswells. Every department gave him ideas. Maybe he could use his partial medical training to take up pharmacy and run a shop that was just as bright and inviting, or a café like the 1738 Tea Room. But the toy department inspired him most. Such colour, such variety, such fun! There was nothing like it in that distant, dusty city and maybe, just maybe, some time in the future, it would join the 21st century and he could open a toy shop there. Ayesha was right; he was a dreamer and as he steered his vacuum cleaner around the merchandise, he dreamed and planned.

Ayesha wasn't waiting either. She had a boyfriend. He was in her accountancy class and eventually summoned the courage to invite her for a coffee. Born on the streets of Mumbai and adopted by a childless couple in Sydney, he recognised her vulnerability and wanted to protect her. They went to bars and music venues but mostly they just talked and walked around that bright and lively city. Their first kiss was an experience beyond anything that Ayesha had ever imagined. She didn't tell Hamid about him.

And Hamid didn't tell her about his next career move. A charity had offered a grant which would enable him to resume his medical education, but the long years of study was now of diminishing appeal. Instead, he set his mind on joining Boswells. Taxi work had given him confidence in dealing with people of all sorts; he had a ready wit and a quick smile. With his dark hair and deep brown eyes he could cut quite a dashing figure. He downloaded an application form from the Boswells website and waited for a vacancy. They didn't seem to come up often.

A few images claiming to be of that distant, dusty city began to appear on social media. The usual blazing buildings and bearded men excitedly brandishing weapons but it was all so tediously familiar. The good doctor managed to power up his phone sufficiently to tell Hamid and Ayesha that water melons were available again and that things were settling down. They weren't, of course. The fateful hour was getting closer and he knew it.

So did everyone else. His extended family kept their distance; lifelong friends avoided him; even his few remaining patients stopped coming. His neighbours began to resent his presence among them. No-one wanted to get caught up in the fate they knew was coming.

After a beery evening with a deafening student band Ayesha and her boyfriend walked home arm-in-arm along the waterfront, the Harbour Bridge towering above them and the lights of the Opera House twinkling in the distance. It was a beautiful, balmy evening and, finding a secluded seat, they held each other closely.

Still no vacancies at Boswells. Hamid had decided that he needed retail experience and wandered morosely round the cavernous Westgate to see if any of the many shops offering employment might appeal. They didn't. At last, a new position was advertised on the Boswells website, and he applied. Of all the occupants in the Littlemore house, he was the first to aim for a job with prospects. His ambition inspired the others and, despite their limited experience and different cultural backgrounds, they set about coaching him in interview technique.

The fateful day arrived. Early evening in Sydney and Ayesha's boyfriend softly closed his bedroom door behind them. It was as spontaneous as it was inevitable. Panic and confusion soon gave way to overwhelming joy.

As the fateful hour approached, Hamid was being interviewed for the vacancy in Boswells. The advertisement said they were 'looking for people with great communication skills and a real passion to deliver great service.' Hamid was just a cleaner but he knew how to charm his interviewers with his dark, smiling eyes and infectious enthusiasm. Politely they listened to his ideas for story-telling in the toy department and cookery demonstrations in the basement and didn't even remind him that the vacancy was in cosmetics and accessories. He was quite right, though; something must be done to draw people in through the Cornmarket entrance and it was useful to know about the floor-covering that had come away in the corner by the saucepans.

And now the fateful time has come.

In that distant, dusty city, wild men smash into the good doctor's flat, drag out his wife and set about him. In less than a minute it is all over.

# Off the Beaten Track

## Annie Winner

The group was the usual mix of bored teenagers and earnest looking tourists. It included a couple of young women, an elderly man with a woman wearing a purple hat, and a smart looking youth with a notebook. Georgie tossed her hair away from her face, switched on her microphone and started her spiel. Her numbers had taken quite a hit since a rival tour provider had taken the concession operating out of the new Boswells coffee shop on Broad Street. She needed to produce some strong performances this week to keep her pitch.

'Welcome everyone. My name is Georgie. I'm about to take you on a fascinating walk. This is a very special tour. We'll explore the side streets and alley ways of this beautiful city, and you'll find yourselves in the famous locations that have featured in the programmes like Inspector Morse, Harry Potter movies and many others. But that's just the half of it. What's special about this tour is that it takes you into some of the ordinary lives of the people who work and shop in Oxford. I think you'll find they are often just as interesting as the more famous characters of both fact and fiction.

You can also buy a copy of this beautiful illustrated map of our route to keep as a souvenir of your visit to Oxford. I should warn you that, as it says in the brochure, this tour includes climbing a few stairs.' She always rushed that last sentence, fearing that it might put people off, or be lost on anyone whose English was bit dodgy.

'Anyone here from the US?' A couple of hands went up.

'Japan?'

'No, China,' muttered one of them, sounding irritated.

'Anyone from Germany?' Another blank.

'Canada?' Nothing.

'Australia?' One.

Georgie's very limited curiosity about her customers was by now exhausted. She had been doing this job on and off for over two years. At the end of every day she wondered how long she could go on churning it out, even though the money was usually pretty good – sometimes well over £200 a day. Perhaps a bit of her didn't really care about her numbers.

'Any questions?'

She had been rattling all this off for so long that she knew the ebbs and flows of the script and when to ignore questions. At this stage people seldom asked any so she usually hardly drew breath before launching into her first object of interest. This time, however, there was a question. It came from a slightly spotty teenage boy with a greasy fringe and huge black glasses. His voice was breaking which made his question sound slightly ghoulish.

'Where were those bishops burnt to death?'

Georgie explained that she would come to that later, but in the meantime she pointed out the cobbled cross in the road opposite Balliol College marking the spot where they had been burned.

Her young questioner persisted.

'How come this is a free tour? It says we only have to give you a tip. How much are we supposed to cough up? Supposing you're crap?' The boy's mother said 'Ssh, Jamie' and took his arm.

'Sorry,' she said, 'he's ….'

Georgie was used to this question and carried on. She knew it all off by heart, Sometimes her mind would wander off on to other planets as she rattled off her script. She would plan her options for tonight's supper or debate with herself whether she could afford to buy the dress she had tried on in Fat Face on her way to work that morning. She tried not to feel weary of this repetitive prattle, and to inject some enthusiasm into her delivery, but she often struggled to concentrate. She sized up her customers again. There were only about twelve of them, predicting a meagre tip take unless she managed to flog more than three copies of the map (in which case she could keep the proceeds).

After her outline of the tour, the estimated ending time, the health and safety mantra, her practised patter began.

'Behind you, to your right, is the magnificent Sheldonian Theatre which was built between 1664 and 1669 and was designed by Christopher Wren. It was paid for by the Archbishop of Canterbury, Gilbert Sheldon (hence the name) and it cost fifteen thousand pounds – nearly two million in today's money. We are going to go up the stairs into the cupola. It's a bit of a climb but you can take it slowly and the view from the top is spectacular. Other points in the street to notice are Blackwell's famous bookshop, founded in 1879. The basement shop is said to cover a quarter of an acre, housing five miles of bookshelves. Then we have the newly-refurbished Weston Library, the Clarendon building, the original Oxfam shop and many other significant structures. We also have the White Horse and the King's Arms pubs and of course the spot where the bishops were burnt in the 16th century. At the end of the street is Boswells department store, in business since 1738, where you can buy almost anything from a suitcase to Lego to a cheese grater. On the corner is Waterstone's, another huge bookshop but a relative newcomer, only in business since 1982. We'll finish the tour here so you will have a chance to explore the shops and the pubs.'

As she explained this Georgie noticed that Jamie looked bored stiff already. She felt a pang of sympathy for him, being dragged round a bunch of tedious old buildings. Crossing the street, she herded the punters up the stairs into the roof space of the Sheldonian. They appeared to be duly impressed by the view, if not by the effort of climbing all those stairs. Even Jamie mustered a bit of curiosity about how the roof was constructed and asked some pertinent questions which Georgie managed to answer to his satisfaction.

ANNIE WINNER

Coming out of the Sheldonian they crossed the street again and carried on past the King's Arms to the Holywell Music Room where the next bit of her script was due. As she finished this she could see Jamie was getting restless again, and his mother more embarrassed. A couple of other members of her flock had slightly glazed expressions too.

With an exhilarating sense of recklessness Georgie found herself launching a different script, one that came from somewhere else inside her brain.

'In the fifth house on the left an infamous crime took place in the 1960s. A young couple who were living here were found dead. The woman had been strangled and the man was hanging from the bannisters. They'd been there for weeks. A neighbour noticed the window on to the street was buzzing with flies and when the police broke in they found their rotting bodies. Turned out the wife had been having an affair, the husband had strangled her and then hanged himself. They had been just about to go on holiday so nobody had noticed their absence for nearly a month'.

Georgie had no idea where this story came from, but she noted a spark of interest flutter across Jamie's expressionless face. Some of the others looked slightly startled, and one of the younger women commented sarcastically to her friend that they were certainly learning something about the ordinary people of Oxford. She led them on into New College, through into New College Lane, along Queen's Lane and on to the High Street, stopping every now and again to return to her text. They crossed the road, dodging the herds of brightly coloured buses, and processed down Logic Lane, a tiny street overhung with ancient houses. Once again Georgie felt herself departing from the trail she was supposed to follow.

'Anybody know what happened here in 1954?' she said. No one answered but Jamie's eyes lit up and his mouth opened slightly.

'Three students were walking down this little lane one evening. It was dark and quite foggy and in those days there was only the light coming down from the main street. They heard what sounded like a clatter of hooves and a clash of swords and suddenly a horseman wearing armour

122

emerged from the gloom and galloped towards them, hotly pursued by another. They tried to flatten themselves against the wall but one of them was knocked to the ground and another felt the sharp tip of a sword penetrate his arm. Only one of them escaped unharmed.'

Georgie paused, searching the faces of her audience. That told her that some were looking sceptical, one man was scribbling in his notebook – but fewer were looking bored.

'So?' said Jamie, a bit truculent.

Georgie just shrugged, suffering an imagination failure, and left his question hanging as she set off again, leading her drove of walkers along Merton Street, up Magpie Lane and back on to the High Street. They crossed the road again and went into the first aisle of the Covered Market.

'This market is among the top ten best markets in the country. It's been going since the 1700s and is home to about 50 small businesses, selling all kinds of food, drinks, clothes, jewellery and much more.' Georgie continued but was interrupted once more by Jamie. She was beginning to feel more than a little irritated by him. He seemed disinhibited in some way and she was beginning to slightly dread what he was going to say next. She was right.

'Why do you think we're interested in a market?' he said, even more truculently. His mother tried to shut him up again, but he ignored her. 'It's no different to any other.' Georgie's briefing – and her experience – had taught her not to respond to hostility. She swallowed, but then again felt swept away from her familiar script.

'This tour promises to show you how the ordinary people of Oxford live,' she said tartly. 'Some of them shop here'.

The sarcasm in her voice temporarily silenced Jamie while Georgie carried on, back along the third aisle, and up the stairs of the Varsity Club. Luckily it wasn't too crowded and the group was able to enjoy the views of roof top Oxford. Jamie looked quite impressed by this, so she ventured a brief exchange with him once she had answered all the questions from the rest of them. These were mostly about what roof

ANNIE WINNER

belonged to which building. Georgie didn't really know most of the time, but she had become pretty adept at making it up – after all most of them wouldn't know any different and they were only in Oxford for a couple of days at the most.

As they went back down King Edward Street and into the back of Christchurch, once again Georgie found herself reeling off the set text, while the other half of her brain was wondering how she could maximise the tips. She really would like to buy the dress she'd seen that morning to wear on her date that evening. He was someone she'd met on Tinder They'd been chatting online for a couple of weeks and had spoken on the phone. Tonight was the all-important first face-to-face encounter.

She was jolted back into the walking tour by one of the college porters asking her to move along to make way for the next group. They left Christchurch through the St Aldates entrance, walking along Brewer Street, past the Dorothy L. Sayers plaque, up St Ebbes Street and along New Inn Hall Street.

Georgie stopped again.

'This house was lived in by the Beatles in the mid-1960s.' she said authoritatively. 'They rented it one summer from Richard Burton and Elizabeth Taylor who bought it as a hideaway during some of the torrid periods of their relationship.'

Jamie interrupted by asking who Richard Burton and Elizabeth Taylor were. Georgie didn't really know herself, but she improvised vaguely that they were film stars at the time which seemed to satisfy him. She continued her fabrication by explaining that the Beatles had written six or seven songs in less than two weeks, smoked an enormous quantity of marijuana and lived on takeaways from a Chinese in George Street. Once again several of her clients looked rather doubtful, and one of them opened his mouth, but something made him think better of it.

'But what I should be pointing out to you is that the building next door was the first Methodist church to be built in Oxford and John Wesley preached here several times – note the plaque behind me'.

'Who's John Wesley?' muttered Jamie. Her group was beginning to look rather disengaged again.

As they reached the junction with George Street the elderly man with the purple-hatted wife told her they were going. He had been having trouble keeping up – the stairs up to the Sheldonian roof, the cobbles of Merton Street and the Varsity Club had finished him off.

'Going back to our hotel,' he said, brandishing a fiver under Georgie's nose. 'Very interesting, but I've had enough.'

Georgie thanked him, secretly quite relieved that she wouldn't have to keep slowing down the group to accommodate his pace, while distinctly underwhelmed by his generosity. She rather half-heartedly tried to sell him a copy of the illustrated map, but he wasn't biting. She hoped the others hadn't seen how stingy he'd been and limit themselves to fivers.

The group followed Georgie through the Gloucester Green market square and into St John's Street. Jamie was getting awkward again, vocalising his boredom to his long-suffering mother. Georgie thought, as she often had before, that this tour was too long.

By now they had progressed along Pusey Street on to St Giles to the Eagle and Child.

'This is where the Inklings used to meet,' she said, 'JRR Tolkien and CS Lewis were the main men, and they were joined by many others'… she just couldn't raise the energy to finish this bit of her script.

The next stop was the Martyrs' Memorial where again Georgie tried to sting herself back into concentrating by recounting the story that at one time students used to get chatting to tourists who were admiring the memorial. The students would tell them that it was the spire to an ancient and beautiful underground church. The entry fee of £5 was then handed over and the hapless tourists were then ushered down the steps to find themselves in the far from fragrant public toilets. Meanwhile the students had legged it.

The final item of the tour was now approaching – the spot-on Broad Street itself where the martyrs were burnt in 1555 and 1556. Georgie always quite enjoyed this bit of the circuit, partly because it was the last stop, but also because it was a stirring tale. She pointed out the plaque on the Balliol wall and gathered her flock round the cross in the road.

'This is the spot on which the Oxford Martyrs were burnt to death on the orders of the Catholic Queen Mary, the daughter of Henry VIII who you might have heard of. They were Hugh Latimer, Bishop of Worcester, and Nicholas Ridley, Bishop of London, executed in 1555 and Thomas Cranmer, Archbishop of Canterbury the following year. They were all Protestants, who were burnt to death for heresy.'

'Ridley suffered a terrible drawn out, agonising death. His brother had bribed the executioner to place gunpowder round his neck to speed things up so he would die quicker but this failed and he endured excruciating pain. The wood was green and burned only Ridley's legs without touching his upper body. Eventually bystanders took pity on him and brought the flames to the top of the pyre to hasten his death. Cranmer was forced to watch the execution and in March 1556 he too was burned at the stake'.

Even though she quite enjoyed the sobering impact this gruesome account had on her audience, she was a bit rattled by the morbid pleasure young Jamie clearly took in the story. Pulling herself back into the end of the tour she said:

'That's it folks. I hope you've enjoyed the tour and the stories and information that you don't get from other walking tours. As you know, this is a free service and I am dependent on how much you kindly contribute.' She looked Jamie in the eye, and he looked away.

'Give her a tenner Mum, that was cool.' Georgie was gobsmacked. There was a murmur of agreement from the group, and they nearly all matched Jamie's Mum's tenner. And seven of them bought the map. After they had drifted off, one of the men in the group returned.

'Not good enough,' he said. His hand went into his breast pocket, whipped out a card and waved it under Georgie's nose. She froze.

'You've deliberately misled our customers and departed from the text. That's in breach of your agreement with Offpiste.'

Georgie was aware of the feeling of a load dropping from her shoulders combined with one of total panic. For the first time that day she didn't know what to say.

'I'm afraid I'm going to have to terminate your relationship with Offpiste immediately. You'd better hand over the maps you haven't sold, and the twenty per cent of the tip take you owe us. Underground church indeed!' As he strode off Georgie became aware that another member of her group had witnessed this exchange.

She stepped up to Georgie and said, 'You did an excellent job on that tour. We're always looking out for guides with a bit of style and imagination. We work out of Boswells Broad Street Café – shall we get a coffee and talk it over?'

As Georgie entertained her date with the story that night, in her new dress, she could hardly stop laughing. 'The underground church scam was the only extra story that WAS true – I got it off Wikipedia!'

# Shopping with Mother
## Neil Hancox

'Do I have to go with you to Oxford tomorrow,' James asked his mother Abby. 'I could stay at home, I have a new computer game to play or I could go…'

Abby cut him short. 'No. Your grandmother has been unwell and she wants to see us both.'

James was silent. He felt the weight of all of his 13 years on his shoulders. There would be two women to look after. Possibly one day adults would understand.

The next morning mother and son were on the train to Oxford. Abby glanced up from the screen of her iPhone where she was pointlessly perusing the world's non-news. James was staring out of the window. She remembered how she had felt at 13, surging hormones and boring adults. She felt a pang of conscience but the boy had to learn that he could not always have his own way.

'Your grandmother has had an operation on her shoulder,' Abby reminded him, 'and she wants to get out for a break, a day of retail therapy.' It was an intriguing expression though truthfully James had a limited idea of what it meant. He knew there were several large department stores in the city and the new Westgate Centre had recently opened but what was the point of walking around them all looking at stuff, commenting, putting the item back, moving on to look at something similar, never buying anything. It was not his idea of therapy.

His mother was fussing. Were those jeans clean? Why wasn't he wearing his new trainers? He instinctively knew silence was golden – what if it rained, he hadn't brought a jacket, where was his handkerchief and was it clean?

The nervous inquisition was interrupted by a voice announcing 'Next station Oxford. If leaving the train here please make sure you have all your bags with you and mind the gap between the platform and the carriage.'

'Time to alight,' James said to his mother, so much better than the phrase 'get off,' he thought. The couple presented their tickets at the automatic barrier and there was grandmother Mary waiting by the information desk. Mother and daughter kissed as mothers and daughters do, he was hugged which spared him some embarrassment. Just in time his grandmother stopped herself saying to him, 'my how you have grown,' though he was by now a gangly youth with untidy hair and a faint fuzz on his chin.

'Good journey?' Mary asked her daughter. 'A bit crowded but we found a couple of seats,' Abby replied.

'I can't think why you didn't drive up, 'Mary said.

Her daughter coloured slightly. 'You know we have only one car now.'

Mary tutted, started to say something about her son-in-law, and then decided to be more conciliatory. 'Let's get going.' She led the trio through the crush at the station entrance, down the steps and past the waiting buses. James was disappointed. He didn't especially like bus journeys, and he had been sitting down for an hour-and-a-half; however, the alternative was walking. Chasing a ball, even restraining the family dog, was one thing. Pavements were tiring with crowds of people and tourists undecided, gazing about them, taking photos. This was an experience he could do without.

They walked on towards the centre of town. Abby was inclined to stride out, her dark hair flopping over her forehead and her glasses repeatedly slipping down her nose. So untidy, Mary thought. Surely she could go to a proper hairdresser and get an optician to make some small adjustment to the frames, but she bit her tongue. Her daughter was sometimes rather touchy.

'Not so fast,' Mary said. Time had not only wearied her, it had slowed her down and shrunk her. She was now a dumpy lady though her white hair still had a mind of its own. A casual observer, however, would have noticed the similarity in jaw line, marking the two women as closely related.

They talked away while James trailed in their wake. They were avoiding cars and vans, narrowly missing bicycles, or should it be the other way around, James wondered, until they were stopped by the lights at the entrance to George Street. After a decent interval the Green Man appeared and they crossed the road, again having to avoid a cyclist who clearly had another interpretation of the Highway Code in mind.

Although James had had a good breakfast and it was ten minutes short of 11o'clock, the cafes and restaurants they passed seemed to beckon to him. His mother and grandmother hurried on until brought up abruptly by more lights and a melee of buses, people and cyclists.

'Where are we going?' James enquired, adding, 'Is it the Westgate Centre?'

'No,' Mary replied. 'Over there, Boswells, the oldest independent department store in Oxford.' James made a mental note of the comment concerning the history of the store. You never knew when such information, tucked away somewhere in a fold in your brain, might prove useful. He remembered he had been there once in the past and visited the toy department on the first floor. There was a model railway that he had found fascinating. Would it still be there? Perhaps his grandmother's choice was a good one. Nowadays though he was past mere toys, he was more interested in computers, games and phones.

As they entered the shop there was one immediate and hopeful sign indicating a tea room on the first floor. James touched his mother's hand, coughed and half whispered, 'Mum, there's a café.' 'Tea Room,' she corrected him. 'And I am sure you and Grandma are dying for a cup of coffee,' he continued. As he spoke, he thought of his new English teacher, a stickler for accuracy. Perhaps dying was not the correct word to use, nevertheless it might do the trick.

There was a brief murmur between the two women and the trio climbed the stairs. James went ahead and found them seats at a window table. They were surrounded by chattering ladies and younger people communing with a laptop or phone. While Mary and Abby studied the menu, although they had already decided on their order, James investigated the cakes arrayed at the entrance to the area. They looked delicious and he had no doubt were delicious, covered in soft icing, sporting strawberry jam and cream between layers of sponge, Danish pastries containing custard and currants, and many more.

A smart young man appeared, and Abby requested two teas, a soft drink and James' choice of cake. The wedge he chose was filled with sweetness and simply asking to be squeezed top and bottom and the filling removed with sweep of the tongue. His mother kicked her son under the table in a half-hearted way without, however, any effect on his behaviour. After 20 minutes, mother and daughter, having veered on to the tendentious subject of James' table manners and uncut hair, decided it was time to move on. Abby paid the bill, 'my treat,' she insisted and serious viewing started.

'What do you want to see?' Mary asked. Abby rummaged in her handbag and extracted a list. 'Kitchen-wear, the non-stick coating on my large pan has virtually gone,' she said. 'Then we need some linen and I must get another suitcase. Before James switched off he had a vision of his being submerged in parcels and bags. Abby would be stressed and bad-tempered and grandmother would be in fussiness overdrive. 'She would be directing operations with comments like watch where you are going, don't let that bag get wet, don't drag it on the pavement...'

Sensing his wilting enthusiasm, though the boy thought he had hidden it very well, Mary turned from her daughter, who was now selecting a small suitcase that would be acceptable to the most contrary of airlines, and said to James, 'where would you like to go?'

He thought for a moment. 'I remember there used to be a toy department,' quickly adding, 'I've grown out of toys, of course, but there might be stuff like Technical Lego. I'll try that.'

With their forces now split, Mary and Abby could argue happily over colours and textures and select birthday and Christmas presents for sundry friends and relatives. 'It may only be July,' Abby said, 'but it's always helpful to have a store of presents on hand, you never know when you might want something in a hurry.' Mary nodded. Her daughter could be sensible at times, even if her judgment was impaired at others.

On the first floor, in the toy department, James was pleased to see plenty of Technical Lego and Engino construction and engineering kits. He examined them with care. Despite his love of computer games and interest in social media these boxes contained exciting promises. Last night his father had given him a tenner. 'Advanced pocket money' his father had called it, no doubt recalling his own forays into the world of soft goods and kitchen-wear when a child. He remembered a world where the exact hue was considered to be so important because of its ability to match the colour of some other article of household apparel, a concept lost, he believed, in children.

The contents of many of the boxes were of too simple a nature for a 13-year old, those he would leave for junior cousins. The technical kits were another matter. With those you could use imagination. There were so many to choose from. Then he noticed the prices and realised that his tenner, even supplemented by pocket money, would not be enough. Wandering into another section of the store he saw competing attractions, especially a 'do-it-yourself' microscope. After some consideration he rejected that in favour of the Lego. Whatever he chose, price was a big problem. Maybe if he played his cards right, meaning exhibiting patience and tact well beyond his years, he could well get a substantial subsidy to augment his total purchasing power. It was certainly worth a try.

A sales lady saw the young boy hovering and asked if he needed help. 'No thank you,' he replied, adding, 'my mum and grandmother will be here soon, when they have finished buying boring stuff like pillow-cases and mugs and saucepans.' The assistant smiled. She recalled what her own children used to think of linen and pots and pans. Strangely, once they had a flat of their own or a partner the attitude changed, which was as well for sales.

James decided on a 'Power Functions' technical kit which he believed he would enjoy. He would keep his fingers crossed that when his grandmother and Abby arrived they would be in a generous mood. Eventually the two women appeared. Grandmother was puffing slightly which was her own fault, her daughter pointed out, since she would not use the lift.

'Is there something you like here?' his mother enquired.

James pointed to a kit in the technical series. 'This looks interesting,' he replied.

Mother and grandmother, oblivious of the engineering excellence and the influence this might have on a developing mind, both looked at the prices. 'Ummm,' was the comment and then, 'How much money have you got, James?'

'Dad gave me a tenner last night,' the boy said, adding 'and I have five pounds of my own.'

His mother wondered at her husband's generosity. She had been told, 'not to forget your credit card,' first thing this morning, with an emphasis on the 'your.'

'It's a lot of money,' Abby observed.

'I've a birthday coming up in a couple of months,' James said.

The words seemed to hang in the air.

Mary nodded. 'It looks exciting to me.'

And what do you know about anything technical, her daughter wondered.

'Alright,' was Abby's eventual verdict.

The item was paid for, a bag was refused and James' reward was placed in the small suitcase his mother had bought downstairs, together with a non-stick pan, a special tin-opener and two pillow-cases. He then had the privilege of towing the suitcase as Abby was now complaining of a headache. The general mood was down. What was needed was another trip to the Tea Room, where with luck they would find a table and catch the tail-end of the lunch menu.

Their fatigue was temporally relieved by a combination of seats and food. Mary announced that she would take a blood pressure pill just in case. Her daughter glared at her. 'You should know by now, Mother, that prescribed medicines should be taken as recommended and not when you feel like it.'

'You have just taken a paracetamol tablet,' her mother replied, 'so don't lecture me.'

The mood changed. It was time to leave. James would have tolerated more shops but the two women were suddenly tired. He towed the suitcase and its contents to Oxford train station where there were placatory kisses and hugs and vaguely sincere exchanges of 'we must do this again.' Abby and James boarded a train while Mary caught a bus to a park and ride from whence a phone call produced, after a 20-minute wait, a husband and car.

'So how did it all go?' her husband asked. Mary kicked off her shoes, remarked that she hoped the kettle was on and that Abby was a fussy soul. 'She can never make her mind up about colours,' Mary said. 'I have no idea where she gets that from.'

'And James, how was he,' Grandfather added.

'He's at that early teenage stage, slightly sullen, and what an appetite.' As they pulled into their driveway Mary's eyes closed.

Indoors she sat down, sighed, accepted the proffered cup of tea and a biscuit. Later that evening she thought, she might give a more detailed account of the day dwelling on her daughter's choice of husband and James' lack of manners. At present she was too tired.

Back at her house, Abby unlocked the door and unpacked her purchases before starting the dinner. 'So how did it go?' her husband asked later.

'I managed to get several things we needed.' James interrupted, 'and I bought a Technical Lego kit.'

Afterwards, when James was in his bedroom investigating his purchase in depth, Abby said to her husband, 'don't you think giving him ten pounds was a bit excessive?' Before he could answer, she added, 'and how did your job-hunting go today?'

Time to change the subject. 'What you need is another glass of wine,' he said. Abby agreed. Perhaps she should have left the topic of her husband's employment for the moment.

She smiled as she sipped a large glass of cold sauvignon blanc, 'And another thing. My mother is so fussy, nothing ever matches, or it's too big or you don't really need it. I think she's getting worse.'

'All in all, a typical day in the life of a nuclear family, warts, Technical Lego, colour matching, relatives and all,' he said.

Abby, relaxed and tired at the same time, groaned and aimed a cushion at her husband's head. 'Don't tell me that you have enrolled in a cod psychology course.'

At that moment James burst into the room, 'I don't follow this instruction, Dad. Can you help?' The phone rang. Abby glanced at the display. It was her mother's number.

'Can I join you on that course?' she asked her husband.

# Oxford in the Time of Cholera

## Jackie Vickers

Mid-morning in Broad Street; late August 1854 and another hot day. Not a cloud in a sky which had been the same deep blue all week. There was a clatter of wheels as a carriage drew up outside Number 46 where Edmund Bevers, surgeon-dentist, had made time to see a distressed young woman who tottered in, her face covered by a scarf. Mr Mucklow, the chemist at Number 25, was measuring out endless potions for a shop full of impatient customers. Elsewhere all was quiet, for most servants had gone early to market to avoid the heat and those residents who could had left town altogether. Frances Holt, highly recommended stay-maker, usually looked forward to this time of year to catch up on her orders, but for days now her damp fingers had slipped on the smooth shiny whalebone so today she crossed the street to gossip with the drapers' assistants at Number 14. For the inhabitants of Dr Acland's house, however, there were few concessions to the weather. Sick patients filled the waiting room and numerous small Aclands galloped around the house, shrieking, to the despair of their nursemaid.

The day had begun badly for Dr Acland with an early call which had taken him out before breakfast. He had insisted the twenty-minute walk would clear his head and refused to take the trap. His patient lived some way along the road to Banbury, adjoining open land, convenient for exercising his dog. Unfortunately, the dog's owner, feeling unwell that morning, had neglected to instruct his staff to attend to the dog and this large, unruly Labrador was now uncontrollable. On hearing the door knocker, the dog had raced along the landing, colliding with the doctor as he reached the top step. His medical bag fell from his grasp, bounced down the entire flight, followed by the delighted dog, who attacked it before the horrified manservant could intervene. The lock was damaged and the contents spread over the tiled hall in the time it took to prise the bag from the over-excited animal. Fortunately, none of the glass phials had broken, but the bag had been damaged beyond repair.

'Such a thing has never happened in all my years of practice,' said Dr Acland, as he sorrowfully examined the torn leather and broken clasp in his consulting room. 'Proof, if any were needed, that such animals should be treated with caution.'

'I will send Liza to Boswells and have them bring a selection of new bags for you to choose from, Henry,' said his wife,

But Henry Acland shook his head. 'I will go myself, before luncheon. I saw exactly the right article in their shop window.'

As soon as breakfast had been cleared, the housemaid went round those rooms which faced the sun, to open windows and draw curtains, in the hope a draught might cool the air. Mrs Acland, a calm and good-natured presence, always busy keeping up with correspondence, teaching the little ones their letters, seeing tradesmen and a series of seemingly endless duties, looked pale and listless. She had given birth to her fourth child not long ago and some said she resumed her tasks too soon. She refused all offers of help, however, and largely ignored her husband's pleas for her to rest, replying with a sweet smile:

'You do not spare yourself, Henry, and my duties are nowhere near as onerous as yours. I know the Good Lord will have endowed me with strength enough to meet my obligations.'

Mrs Acland did, however, concede that as their cook was exceptionally competent, she could and would, allow her to take over planning and organisation of all the meals. No small task, as there was an endless stream of friends and acquaintances regularly pressed into joining the family at meals.

That morning Esther, the new kitchen maid, rushed through the back entrance, shaking and shrieking. Cook acted quickly to contain the noise in those rooms by the kitchen. With all the hustle and bustle within the house, doors slamming and children shouting, no-one heard the commotion. Esther Marsh was eighteen and a recent addition to the household and given to hysterical outbursts. Cook had told the other servants that although the new maid was prone to fits of 'nerves', she was none the worse for that.

'I've sin many worse. She'll soon shape up given time and space.' But this morning's upset was worse than usual, and it took all Cook's skill to calm her down. Sensing trouble, the servants gathered round to watch. With some sniffing and taking many gulps of water, Esther explained.

'I saw some early greengages this morning and Cook sent me back to get some because Mr Ruskin's coming for supper and he's very partial. But they must've sold out, or I got in a muddle about where I'd sin 'em.'

The old gardener rolled his eyes and Esther flew at him. 'It's difficult to get yer bearings, George Mason, when yer new to a place. I'd like to see you do any better.'

Cook shook her head and glared at the old gardener. 'Go on.'

'A woman next to me said there was better apples in Gas Street and then another woman said as you'd be mad to go down Gas Street as there were three down there had the cholera. And that's not counting those in the prison what backs onto it.'

Liza the housemaid said she heard a man was ill in Jericho. 'They said it started there last time.'

'So, what made you run back then? And without them plums?' Cook asked Esther.

'I know a lot of folk died last time and I got frit thinking of home and was they alright?'

'A lot of fuss about nothing,' muttered George.

'And that doesn't help, George Mason,' snapped Cook, herself unsure whether or not to sympathise with Esther. 'Look,' she said, patting the girl's shoulder, 'your family are out in the country, miles away from all this illness. Stop worrying about them. You don't see Dr Acland fretting over his little ones and they're only streets away from the cholera.'

'You knew!' Esther jumped up and glared at Cook. 'You knew and said nothing.'

'Do you wonder?' laughed Liza, 'the commotion you make.'

'There's nothing we can do,' said Cook. 'You get it or you don't. What's the good of getting in a lather. Now, I've no more time to waste, there's dinner to get going and this heat's getting worse. Now, Esther, I want you to …'

But Esther, sobbing, had rushed up the back stairs.

'That girl,' sighed Cook.


By mid-day Mrs Acland and Jane, the nursemaid, had taken all the children to have a picnic by Norham Manor. Dr Acland was out seeing patients so Cook put out cold left-overs, but the heat was such that the servants mostly picked at their food. Esther had not appeared since mid-morning.

'Knows she made a spectacle of herself. Sulking I shouldn't wonder.'

'Well, never mind, Liza. You go and see she's alright.'

Esther was not in her room and Liza declared it was much too hot to go looking, so they let her stew. By two o'clock Cook grew restive and went up herself to Esther's room. Her uniform lay on the bed; shoes and shawl were missing.

'I wonder,' murmured Cook. Listlessly she looked around and then out of the window down at the garden below where George Mason was sweeping the paths. Distant sounds of children re-energised her. They would be back soon for drinks and naps and the house would begin to fill up with patients once more. Cook rapidly rolled up a blanket and stuffed it under the bedspread. She folded the black dress and put it on the chair and closed the curtains. Esther was small and slight, surely the shape in the bed would pass muster in the gloom.

'She's got a headache,' she told the rest of the staff. 'Too much sun, I shouldn't wonder. We'll just leave her be.'

It was not until the evening supper was cleared that Liza began to grumble about Esther. 'It's all extra for us.'

Then George joined in. 'One short and it's us that suffers. Always t' same for t' workers.'

'And when did you last really exert yourself George Mason?' snapped Cook, 'You're not one to talk. Do you know where the Doctor was last night? He was called out to Jericho, two o' clock, I heard him go. And taking prayers at 7.00, out again before breakfast and a waiting room full by 8.30. In all my years in service I have never seen anyone work like him. All day, some of the night and most weekends. Church on Sundays his only time off. And before you say – he cares as much for the poor of this parish as he does the rich. A few years ago Dr Liddell was on at Mrs Acland about how ill and tired he looked and how she should try to get him to take a year off. He's lucky if he gets a week off. So, don't ever let me hear you say such rubbish again. Not in my kitchen!' Cook flung her apron aside and stormed out.

There was an uneasy pause. 'Reckon she's right, mostly,' George conceded, 'though she be a bit partial to the good Doctor, we all know that!'

The following day there was still no sign of Esther but Cook managed to keep up the pretence that the housemaid needed to rest. By late afternoon Liza was becoming suspicious, despite Cook's assurances. In the end Cook took her aside.

'She'll never get another place as good as this, and who knows what's going on. We can keep it up till morning, then it'll be up to her.'

The next morning, work stopped suddenly at the unusual sight of Dr Acland, one hand on the door-knob, leaning into the kitchen, his gaunt features looking more tired than usual.

'Mrs Rayment, I have not seen Esther these three days.'

'She must have caught a chill, Sir.' Cook looked in his direction but did not meet his gaze.

'I should see her without delay, in that case. To catch a chill during a heat-wave is unusual and merits my interest.'

'I'm sure she will be better soon.' Cook's face was red and blotchy. She turned back to her pans and began stirring each in turn. She glanced over her shoulder, but he was still in the doorway. 'Is there anything else, Sir?'

'Yes, indeed. You can show me up to Esther's room, if you please. I cannot have one of my servants neglected.'

'But…'

'Mrs Rayment!' he raised his voice. 'There is cholera in this town. I need to see Esther.'

'Well, I'm sure she hasn't got cholera, Sir.'

Dr Acland nodded, suppressing a smile. 'Suppose we get a second opinion?' he said and followed her up the back stairs.

Perhaps Cook accepted she had lost the battle, or perhaps it was the thought of having left her cooking unattended, but she raced up the two flights of stairs, knocked on the nearest door and went in without waiting for a reply. Esther was sitting on the bed in her outdoor clothes, taking off some very dusty shoes. Around lay various packages loosely tied with string.

'As you say,' murmured the doctor, 'Esther clearly does not have cholera. I will see her in my consulting room presently.'

'Now look what a pickle we're in' hissed Cook after the doctor had gone. 'Where've you bin?'

'I bin back 'ome.' Dark rings circled her eyes which stared out from a grimy face.

'Well, get yourself cleaned up, girl, and think of some excuse, else you'll lose your place and you'll never find one as good.' A strong smell of overdone vegetables rose up from the kitchen. Cook gave a cry of alarm and disappeared down the stairs.

The waiting room was full, as usual, but Doctor Acland called Esther in as soon as she appeared, presentable now in her black dress and starched apron.

'I 'ad to go 'ome, Sir,' said Esther, knowing it was hopeless trying to deceive her employer. 'And I'm ever so sorry,' she added.

'Why did you run off? Are you not happy here?' Acland looked mystified rather than angry and Esther managed to swallow back her tears.

'Because of the cholera. I was worried about the family back 'ome. They 'ad it bad in some of the country towns, five year ago. I can remember it well, we was all worried then. And now I feel it more c'os…' She looked down at her hands, smoothing her apron over and over.

'Why do you feel it more?' There was no reply, so Acland tried again. 'How many are there in your family?'

'There's only two of the eight of us left at 'ome, but there's mother and little Charlie. Only little 'e is.' She sniffed.

'I thought you were the youngest of eight?' said the doctor, who always remembered every last detail about his staff.

'Mother 'ad another.' She paused, then added, 'after a big gap.'

Doctor Acland sighed. 'How old is your mother's eldest? 30?'

'Well, past 35,' said Esther, looking confused.

'Esther,' the doctor said gently, 'your mother is much too old to have had another baby. Did you think I wouldn't know that?' He waited a few moments but Esther said nothing. 'I think she is bringing up someone else's child. Someone very close to her perhaps?' Esther nodded. 'Is little Charlie your child?'

The tears welled up and began to roll down Esther's face. 'It's so 'ard, leaving 'im there. Not but what 'e isn't cared for really well. Mother treats 'im just like 'er own. An' that's 'ard an all. Then when I 'eard about the cholera I just panicked. I won't be seeing 'im for months, unless Mother can come down with the carrier, she said she might.'

Doctor Acland leaned forward. 'Now look at me, Esther. Your family live out in the country, somewhere near Banbury, well away from polluted wells, choked-up sewers and crowded housing. Little Charlie will be quite safe. No need for you to run off in a panic. Cook can't manage without you, you know.' He sat back and started re-arranging the papers on his desk, his expression suddenly stern. 'But what of the father?'

Esther's face lit up. ''e's a stonemason, Sir. You should see his carving. ''e's working on one of the colleges at the minute, an' they do think a l'ot of 'im. Wonderful work, they all say.' She looked down at her hands again. 'But I aven't told 'im.'

'I think he might be proud to have a son, Esther. You should tell him. And he should marry you. There are worse things to be than a skilled mason in Oxford these days. There may be much work soon...'. He stopped, smiling to himself, some private thought stirred him, and he strode to the door. 'You may find you do not need to be a live-in servant for many more years.'

After Esther had left, he rummaged through some papers until he found a large sheet folded many times. He straightened it and allowed himself a few minutes to gaze at a sketch of a large and imposing building entitled 'Front elevation of proposed museum'. Below it was a plan showing a massive exhibition hall with galleries. 'There will be work for Esther's stonemason and many more when this project gets underway.'

The next hour or so was spent dealing with people in various stages of illness: those he could help, and those he could not. Eventually his last patient came in. She rummaged in her bag and put a bottle down on his desk.

'How is your cough, Mrs Dewhurst?'

'Quite gone, thank you Doctor.'

'So, how can I help you?'

'I heard the cholera was back, so I went to Mr Johnson, the chemist up our way, and he gave me this. You soak your handkerchief and hold it to your nose. Only my Joshua laughed at me. Said Johnson had taken good money off me for aniseed cordial, what will do no good. Can it stop the cholera, Doctor?'

Dr Acland unscrewed the top. As he sniffed the bottle, a strong smell of aniseed filled the room.

'Dear me, Mrs Dewhurst! I fear Mr Dewhurst is quite right. For a long time people believed a 'miasma' to be the cause of contagion, but a Dr Snow, in London, has good evidence that sewage and foul water is more of a threat. As you live on Boars Hill, where both air and water are pure, you need have no fear. Keep away from St Ebbes and the other low-lying areas until the epidemic is over. And, if you need a chemist, The Oxford Drug Company will never sell you questionable products. Ask for Mr Pearson.'

The waiting room was now empty, but, like the consulting room, reeked of aniseed. Mrs Dewhurst, being his last patient, had been demonstrating Mr Johnson's 'cure' to a room full of sick and apprehensive patients.

Henry Acland called to Liza. 'I want every member of my household to come to this waiting room immediately.'

Within minutes all the servants had assembled. Dr Acland stood before them, hands behind his back, as though about to address his students in the university.

'I do not have to tell you that there is cholera in Oxford, once more. There is no need for alarm if you follow these simple rules which will keep us all safe from infection.'

Then Henry Acland explained clearly and simply that clean water from their own well, fresh air and personal hygiene were what was required. He mentioned briefly the new ideas from London, proposed by a Dr Snow, that pollution from sewage was a more likely cause of the disease than foul air.

'The important thing,' he said, pacing up and down, 'is that you do not listen to gossip. Unscrupulous shopkeepers may produce worthless concoctions. A chemist, to the west of this city, is peddling essence of aniseed. You may have noticed the odour in this room. On no account should anyone here allow themselves to be tempted by this, or any other, charlatan. There are several reputable pharmacies in Broad Street and beyond. So, to conclude, at this time there is no known cure for cholera. We must depend on cleanliness, good nursing and, as always, prayer.'

At this prompting, all the servants and Mrs Acland stood, bowed their heads and were led in prayer by their employer.

Dr Acland returned to his consulting room to prepare for the day's visits. He checked the contents of his new medical bag, noting with satisfaction that the layout was an improvement on his old one. 'Quite a satisfactory outcome,' he thought, 'I have acquired the latest in medical bags and the obliging Mr Boswell has made a good sale. Furthermore, when the unfortunate patient is presented with the bill, he will perhaps reflect that the whole sorry affair had originated in his own over-indulgence in champagne and oysters the night before.'

There was to be no respite for Dr Acland and the other doctors, nurses and helpers who worked tirelessly in the worst affected parts of Oxford, mainly in the parishes of St Ebbes and St Thomas, in the following weeks. It was generally thought to be to everyone's advantage that the young gentlemen from the colleges would be away till October. However, for those who depended on the university for employment, this summer was, as every summer, a difficult time. Dr Acland was concerned that the undernourished would this year be more vulnerable to infection, but when he approached Christ Church, they put their kitchens at his disposal, enabling quantities of broth to be dispensed to the poor and thus saving lives. As the authorities were loth to contribute, Acland and his friends supported these measures from their own pockets. Of the 319 that caught the disease in Oxford, 200 died, but by the end of October the cholera had run its course.

# Coming Together?

## Geoff Bremble

Henry was sitting alone in his usual spot in Boswells Tea Room. It was near closing time and all the other customers had left, allowing Molly time to complete her cleaning up before the two of them could leave for home. He'd purchased the Daily Mirror on his way there and, after devouring the sports pages, was flicking through the rest of the paper. He got to page three and stared in total disbelief. There, before his eyes, was a younger him staring out from behind a pixelated face. But it was definitely him with a bride on his arm under a headline banner

Queen Elizabeth & Henry VIII
Bigamist Bride Released

He started to read the report. 'Elizabeth Trump has been released from prison having gained notoriety by marrying eight men all named Henry over a period of 15 years, seven of them bigamously. It is understood that she has a two-year-old boy, also named Henry, the father being her last victim and who became known as Henry VIII…'. It was definitely her. How could he forget her ghostly, elf-like features, jet black hair and piercing green eyes coupled with an underlying sadness and quiet demeanour? Henry held the image for a moment or two before closing the newspaper and sat, staring straight ahead, his heart racing.

'You alright Henry?' asked Molly, the Tea Room manager who he had been living with for just under two years. She was a short, heavy woman, used to getting her ways and with a Scouse accent which became evident on those few occasions when she felt someone was having a go at her. Henry was a couple of inches taller than her, slim and of an easy-going disposition and people often wondered how the two had got together, but there was no doubt who ruled the roost.

'Henry, what is it?' exclaimed a now worried Molly.

'Nothing,' mumbled Henry as he slid off his seat, leaving his coffee and the newspaper on the table. He went down the stairs and crossed the floor before stepping out into Broad Street. He then turned left and, with his heart still pounding he walked on unseeing towards Cornmarket.

'God alive, she's out. I didn't know she was still in there. The bitch, she should have got life for what she did to me.' Then came another thought, 'Bloody hell, what would I do if she came to find me? After all, that's what she said she'd do when she was sentenced. Said she still loved me and could I forgive her,' he paused.' Not a chance. She can rot in hell as far as I'm concerned.'

By this time his heart had returned to an almost normal beat and he turned on his heel, heading back to Boswells. He sat down at his still empty seat, newspaper and coffee still there. Molly hurried over,

'Henry. What was that all about? I'm almost finished – then we can go.'

'I'm OK. I just came over a bit weird and needed to get some fresh air. But you'd better see this,' he said as he unfolded the Mirror.

She looked at the photograph of him and his bride and started to read the account of how he had been the eighth Henry to marry her. One particular sentence caught her eye 'this heartless woman ruined the lives of so many men, marrying them for the lottery money each one had had the fortune to acquire.'

'It's you isn't it? What does this mean? Are you still married to her?'

'Yes, it's me and no, we're not still married. I was never married to her. Bigamous marriages aren't legal and I want nothing more to do with her. I didn't tell you about her because there was nothing to tell.'

'Oh, you poor thing, getting mixed up with a harlot like that. Women of her kind should get all the punishment they deserve.'

'Well that's a bit unfair,' said Henry, 'she didn't exactly ruin my life and it was fun while it lasted. At least she didn't get her hands on my money and now I'm more than happy with you.'

'Come here, you poor man. Let me give you a hug,' Molly said as she took him in her arms, a smile on her face.

A couple of days later back at Boswells Henry was seated in the Tea Room, which was about to close, and Molly was in the kitchen. He suddenly felt a vice-like grip on his shoulder, a grip not unlike a policeman's grip would be in the event of an arrest.

'Alright our kid. How you doing? Long-time no-see.'

Henry immediately recognised the strong Scouse accent even though it had been over three years since he had last heard it. He turned round to find a rugged, unshaven, six-feet four-inches tall Liverpudlian towering a good two inches over him. He remembered him as a kind, outgoing man, who had tried to cheer him up after being told about how he had been caught up in the infamous bigamy trial ten years earlier. But at this moment this was the last voice he wanted to hear.

'What are you doing here and how did you find me?' he asked with a touch of panic.

'Easy. The 'Pool are playing Oxford again so I 'ad to come down and, having read a couple of days ago in the Mirror about you and you know who,' he paused, 'I assume you've seen it, and dat she's gorr'a kid,' then, satisfied that Henry had seen, it Billy carried on, 'well I decided to look you up. Finding you was easy as pie, I asked at de Gloucester, dey told me you'd gone teetotal and would be 'ere, so 'ere I am.'

'Of course I've read it. What's it to do with you?' Henry snapped.

'Well dat's a long story but, before I tell it, ow about standing me a coffee. Der's still time I tink.'

By this time Molly had sidled over and had caught Billy's last few words. He was sitting with his back to her so she was unable to see his face, but his voice gave her a feeling that she ought to know him. Henry turned towards Molly and gave her Billy's order.

'And you Henry my love?' she managed to ask, her voice quivering.

'Thanks Molly but no thanks,' and, to Molly's disappointment Henry turned to Billy and suggested they move to a table by the widow. It was then, seeing the newcomer towering over Henry, that she realised she had plenty to worry about.

Once settled down Billy opened up. 'You remember arr conversation dat day when all the news broke and she'd been collared? How you said she was a bit of a lewker and you still fancied 'er, even after all she'd done. Well, when I got back 'ome I got round to think'n about what made her do it. So I decided to trace her and ger 'er side of the story.'

'That was nice of you,' Henry responded facetiously.

'Alright, I know she's the last person you wanna hear about, but things have changed.'

'Get on with it then, tell me what's changed that's so important that you've come down all this way just to see me,' retorted Henry.

'I went to one of de 'earings, found she was staying with friends while waiting for der trial, and followed her. Lucky for me it was up near Liverpool. I contacted 'er and at first she said no but when I said I knew you and we were in touch she agreed to meet me.'

'But that wasn't true. I haven't seen or heard from you since that day in the Gloucester, I didn't even know your name.'

'Well what's one more lie after all de other's dat she'd told. Anyway, it got me in and my charming manner soon won her over and den one thing led to another and de next th'n she was preggers.'

'Congratulations, but I still don't see what all this has got to do with me.'

'Well, der was only two months between you two splitting, 'er getting banged up and me in between, so obviously der's some question as to who de dad might be.'

'That's ridiculous and anyway I don't want anything to do with her or any kid that may or may not be mine.'

'Hang on, it doesn't finish 'ere. I kept in touch with 'er when she was inside and then, when she gorr out, she moved in wid me on a temporary basis, no hanky-panky you understand and now she says she wants to know who de father is.'

'So?' responded Henry, 'Just tell her it's not me. Tell her I'm impotent, that should do it. As you said what's another lie?'

'Sorry, dat won't wirk, she decided to do a DNA test on you, me and de kid.'

Henry went silent and Billy allowed him time to take in the implications of this new situation.

'I can see how she got yours and the boy's DNA but how did she get mine?' muttered Henry now realising that this nightmare was not going away.

'Do you remember you told me dat she gave you a lock of 'er 'air to set in a pendant on a chain? As a love token for you to wear.'

'Yes,' Henry responded guardedly.

'And then she cut a lock of yer 'air. Saying it was so she could 'ave you near 'er always.'

'Yes,' responded Henry beginning to sense that he was going to hear something he didn't want to hear.

'Well she used dat?'

Henry went hot then cold. He wasn't sure whether to laugh or cry.

'I don't believe it,' was all he could muster.

'It's true, and she'll be 'ere around six o'clock when all will be revealed. It could be you. It could be me.'

Henry stared at Billy lost for words and, slowly leaning forward, he rested his head on the table, 'Me, why me?' he groaned.

Billy stood up, and patted Henry gently on his back, 'She'll be here any time now and she's got the boy and 'er gran with 'er. I'll go down and meet 'er and I want no messing about from you. I don't want to find you've done a runner when we get back.'

Henry sat up and watched as Billy disappeared downstairs. Ten minutes went by, then 20, before Billy returned followed by she who had been his wife. She was as beautiful as he remembered, her outfit still immaculately stylish. She spotted Henry and gave him a questioning smile. His heart leapt, he didn't know why. It was then that Molly appeared from the kitchen with Billy's coffee. Then she saw him. It was Billy who spoke first, 'What the hell are you doing here?'

'I could ask the same about you,' was Molly's sharp retort still holding the coffee.

'It's none of your f'ing business,' Billy snarled back.

Molly, having a good idea about what lay ahead immediately went on the offensive. 'Wherever that business is,' she said, immediately turning towards Lizzie, 'it won't be in your interest, it's himself he's thinking about, not you.'

'Dat's a lie,' Billy snapped back 'and I'm sure it's not by accident dat you're 'ere. After Henry's thousands are yous?'

'What thousands? I dunno' know what you're talking about,' Molly returned.

'Too bloody right you do. Have you told him about how you come to know Lizzie?' said Billy turning towards Henry, 'Visited inmates in de prison dat Lizzie was in, made friends wid 'er, knows all about you and little Henry. Told you dat has she? I bet she hasn't and it's no coincidence dat she dumped me as soon as Lizzie told her about you and all your money,' He turned towards Molly, 'I wondered where you'd gone, now I know, down here to get yer' hands on me-lado's cash.'

'Don't you believe him,' said Molly as she turned to Lizzie. 'We'd been going along nicely until he found out from you about little Henry. It was him who dumped me to take up with you, probably figuring out there would be a chance of selling his story to the papers about his life with a famous bigamist. And I bet he's been working on how he could find out if the kid was Henry's,' then she paused in her tirade,' or has he already found out. He has hasn't he, and he's down here to help you get Henry's money. A bloody gold-digger, never done an honest day's work in his life, lived off the dole and whoever he could con. If truth be told I was glad to see the back of him.'

Billy, aghast at this interpretation of his relationship with Lizzie tried to defend himself, 'You bitch, you know dat's a pack of porkies. I'm not like dat, a bit of a jack-of-all trades but I've never taken advantage of a woman or anyone else in my life, and you know dat.' He turned to Lizzie, 'it's not true what she's saying. You do believe me don't yer?'

Hearing all this, Henry didn't know what to believe. He looked towards Molly, pleading for an explanation but her silence told him all he needed to know. She pulled a face and disappeared back into the kitchen. He turned towards Lizzie now knowing he had to find the truth from her. Suddenly Lizzie sprang into life, 'Stop it, stop it. I don't want to hear any more,' she screamed as she stood up and turned to leave the room. Henry sprang into action. He grabbed her arm and dragged her towards the stairs before racing them down to the basement. Once there he hesitated before turning left and, spying what seemed like a storage room with its door slightly open, pointed Lizzie in its direction.

'Quick, get in there and keep out of sight. I'll go and see where the other two are.'

He closed the door behind her and moved gingerly up the stairs back to the ground floor. When he was confident that neither Billy nor Molly were looking for them, he went back to Lizzie. She hadn't spoken a word since her outburst and was still in a state of shock. Henry sat down beside her and put his arm around her.

'Come on,' he said, 'I think it's safe, I'm sure they're not after us but why did you do it? Seven marriages and only one legal. Then left me when I wouldn't open a joint account and I know you've got a kid. Who the hell are you?" he asked, now with no anger in his voice.

'You, I didn't mean to hurt you,' she said, her eyes welling up with tears, let me explain. I didn't leave because of the money. I left because I saw one of my exes here, in Boswells. I just panicked, ran away and went up north as far away as possible.'

'So, what about Billy, where does he fit in?'

'He's obviously told you how he found me and that we immediately got on well with each other.'

'Yes, he told me what happened.'

'I just needed a bit of loving and he was there,' she responded defensively. 'When I went into prison we kept in touch and he visited me every so often. I told him about how much I liked you. I was beginning to realise that of all my husbands you were the only one who was sweet and kind and had never spoken a harsh word to me. Yes, you were gullible, and I took advantage of you, but the memory of how kind you'd been made me want to see you again. I was planning to get in touch with you when the law caught up with me.'

'That was three years ago and you expect me to believe that. You could have written,' interrupted Henry.

'You wouldn't have believed me. I knew I would have to see you face-to-face to explain, but that became impossible.'

'And, Billy what happened next?'

'When I was released he took me and little Henry in, as lodgers, nothing else. It was he who persuaded me to come and see you, see if we can't at least be friends again.'

'Alright, I believe you. God knows why. So where does Molly fit in.'

'As Billy said, she was a prison visitor. I only saw her a few times and I'm sure that the last time she saw me was just after Henry was born.'

Henry sat back, thinking while Lizzie waited for a reaction.

'Do you believe Molly, about Billy?' he asked.

'No, not at all. Billy's one of those who lives from day-to-day, never thinks about the future and never asked me about you or the others or the money.'

'And Billy, about Molly?'

'Yes, every word, I'm sorry'

It was then that Henry came to the crunch.

'Is it true what Billy says, you've done a DNA test on the both of us and the kid? Do you know who the father is?'

Lizzie paused before answering.

'No, I don't, but I have an envelope with the results inside but I haven't opened it yet,' she paused, 'maybe we should go upstairs before we do anything, after all Billy has a right to be there when we get the results.'

They moved back up and found Billy in the Tea Room having been joined by little Henry and Lizzie's Gran. There was no sign of Molly.

Little Henry ran over to his mother, Henry introduced himself to Lizzie's gran and then they all sat down. It was Lizzie who spoke first, explaining about the contents of the envelope she was holding in her hand, then continued, 'And now it's time to open the envelope and as Gran's not involved in our little triangle she can do it. But before she does, can I say that you two are the kindest, gentlest and most honest men I've ever known, and I love you both to bits. Now Gran here's the envelope. Would you open it please?'

Gran carefully did as she was told and looked inside. There was no document. She immediately looked towards Lizzie questioningly. Lizzie nodded. She then poured the contents of the envelope onto the table. It was a mixture of tufts of hair, the fair ones obviously Henry's, the ginger ones Billy's and the black ones Lizzie's. There was a shocked silence at this revelation which was exacerbated by Lizzie's next words.

'Sorry, boys. Let me explain. When I was going to do the DNA test I found out that cut hair can only be used to determine the maternal line. For the paternity line you need a follicle attached to the hair, which of course I didn't have. This set me thinking as to whether I really needed to know who Henry's dad was. Then I decided I didn't need to. I realised I love both of you and it's both of you I want to be with. So, what do you say?'

There was a shocked silence in the room, little Henry started to cry, Gran picked him up and without saying a word made her way to the stairs wondering what to make of what had just happened and, more importantly, what was going to happen next.

# A Change of Heart

## Jenny Burrage

Amy knew she had taken completely the wrong job. She had worked in McCauley's transport office for two years now since leaving school.

She hated it. When she woke each morning, she had a strong desire to pull the covers over her head and pretend she didn't have to go there. The lives of lorries, buses, trucks and all the vehicles on four or more wheels dominated her working life. She hadn't even learned to drive and still lived with her parents.

'You are a complete wimp, Amy,' she told herself. 'Sitting at that desk surrounded by reams of paper and files. Isolated for all hours of the day. Wondering what it would be like down the corridor in the bustle and noise of the main office. Stupid, stupid. Get a life, girl.'

'I know,' she said to her reflection in the mirror in the ladies, 'I'm going to leave this crappy job ASAP.' Her reflection smiled back, nodding in approval.

That evening she told her long-time boyfriend, Canadian-born Luke, what she had decided. They'd met when he joined her school in the sixth form. His parents had been in Oxford two years, they had returned to Canada recently and he had stayed on.

'Are you sure, Amy?'

Of course, she was sure. Why was he always so careful about everything? No spirit of adventure. Sometimes she felt like shaking him.

'Sleep on it.'

'No. I've made up my mind. Really and truly.' She could see him frowning. She loved him of course and so did her family.

'He's a lovely boy. You hang onto him,' Gran told Amy.


Next day, just before home time, there she was standing in the chief's office, resignation letter in her hand. She hadn't sat in the same chair since she was interviewed. She remembered how she felt sitting in that chair then and she still had the same feeling now. Scary. She stood behind it, waiting.

The boss appeared. Ben Wilson was new, hadn't been in the job long. He'd always appeared so far above her, status-wise, and she hadn't come into contact with him much. She had to admit he was very good looking.

'Hello Amy and what can I do for you?' He smiled, indicating the chair.

She ignored it and plonked the letter on the table. 'I'm leaving, Mr Wilson. This is my resignation.'

He stared at her, smile now vanished. 'May I ask why?'

'I need a change.'

'I see. Is that the only reason?'

'Yes.'

'I hope you will think again. There is a new post coming up, a branch assistant, working on the trade counter and in our store. You would be talking to people, a very different position from the one you have at the moment. I realise you have been rather isolated in that small office.'

She stared back at him. She hadn't expected this. Thoughts whirled round and round.

'Will you think about it, Amy?' He offered her back the letter. 'I don't want to lose you.'

'Thanks, but I've made up my mind.' She put the letter once more back on his desk and that was it.

She decided to walk into Oxford to catch the bus home. She needed to clear her head. Something didn't seem right. She really liked the new boss, and there he was offering her promotion. She felt pleased about that. Her mobile rang, it was Mum and back to reality.

'Amy, where are you?'

'Oh, hello Mum. In the city centre. Just on my way to get the bus home.'

'I wondered if you'd remembered it's Grandad's birthday tomorrow.'

'Oh no. I'd totally forgotten. Lucky you phoned.'

'He and Gran and Luke are coming over tomorrow for tea. Your dad will join us later on. Can you get Grandad something in Oxford? He'd love a small present from you, like always.'

'Yes. I know the very thing. Thanks Mum. Bye. See you soon.'

But as it turned out, Amy didn't go home soon. Something happened. Unexpected.


'Dear Grandad', she thought as she made her way to Boswells. She wandered in and found the place she wanted on the ground floor. She smiled as she thought of Grandad's face if he knew she was going to buy him something from the cosmetics department. She'd seen the item at Christmas when she was buying some perfume as a present. Grandad, she'd thought at the time. Perfect. It was still there, thank goodness, a small gold tin of soap scented with whisky, manufactured in Scotland of course. Unusual, she thought, and it would make him laugh. She almost laughed out loud herself and then she realised she had momentarily forgotten her ordeal. As she reached for the tin, she sensed there was someone at her shoulder. She turned.

'Mr Wilson.'

'Call me Ben, please. Sorry if I startled you.'

'What are you doing here?'

'I feel a bit like a stalker, Amy. I followed you, wanting a chance to speak to you, away from McCauleys.'

'But why? I don't understand.'

'Of course, you don't. I owe you an explanation.'

'Well, go on then.'

Again, her mind was in a turmoil. Then the fatal smile from Ben was there.

'Look, Amy, not here, I need to talk to you over a coffee. Is that OK?'

'I must pay for this first.' She held up the tin.

'Of course.'

She was flattered, fumbled for her credit card, wondering where all this was leading.

By then, the tea room upstairs had closed so, ten minutes later, there they were sitting in Costa in the Clarendon Centre, drinking espressos. Ben stared into his coffee, and Amy – well, now she felt she was her own person, not nervous at all. So, where's this leading she asked herself ....

'Go on then, Ben.' To her surprise she found calling him Ben easier than she'd thought.

He slowly looked up and, smiling again, leaned across the table and took her hands in his.

'The first day I started work at McCauley's, I was nervous. It was a big responsibility and so many staff to oversee.'

'Yes, but what has that got to do with me leaving?'

'Everything. You see the minute I saw you, I fell in love.'

'What?'

'Love, Amy. Love. With you.'

She felt tears pricking at her eyes, her pulse racing, alive to the moment.

'You aren't married then, Ben?'

'Thirty-five and single.' He kissed her softly on the lips and she responded, her body tingling. So, this was where it was leading.

'Mmmm,' she said.

'Well now you know all. I couldn't approach you. It would have been 'inappropriate', me the new boss and all that, but when you told me you were leaving, I had to do something.'

'I suppose so. But now?'

He kissed her again. 'We shall keep it secret, my darling Amy. That is if you feel the same way about me.'

She knew she did. How it had happened was inexplicable and she felt her hands reaching for his. This was truly love at first sight. She'd always thought that was so untrue … but now …

'I think I do,' she said. 'And I will take the new post you offered me.'

'That's wonderful. Come on then, Amy,' he said. 'I shall walk you back to base to pick up my car and then I shall drive you home.'

But there was no going home at that point in the evening.

Ben took her back to his flat in a shabby somewhat run-down area. She noticed it was a typical bachelor place, untidy, but surprisingly cramped for a presumably well-paid boss with a new Mazda sports car.

'Sorry it's a bit of a tip,' he said.

'No worries,' she told him. He pulled her towards him and took her in his arms and moved his hands under her shirt. She melted under a long kiss.

The double bed almost filled the tiny bedroom and this was where Amy spent the next few hours. She had never felt like this before. Ever.

Ben eventually dropped her off at home long after midnight.

'Amy?' she heard as she opened the front door.

'Sorry, Mum. Go back to bed.' There was no need for an explanation. She sometimes came home late when she was with Luke. Her Mum always appeared when she was later than usual. She didn't seem to realise her daughter was twenty. Luke … she felt guilty that she hadn't thought of him once while she was with Ben. She made for her bed and was fast asleep before she had time to dwell on boyfriend problem.

Grandad's tea party, next day, which started at six o'clock so everyone could get there after work, went well. Grandad opened the little tin of whisky scented soap and sniffed.

'Well it looks good and it smells good, but I don't think I'd better taste it,' he said. Everyone laughed. Luke scanned the contents on the back of the tin.

'It's definitely got whisky extracts,' he said.

'I've never seen anything like that before,' said Gran.' Whatever next will they think of?'

Luke gave Grandad a bright blue muffler and a tin of Canadian maple syrup.

'Thank you all. What a lucky chap I am,' he said.

After the birthday meal, Amy volunteered to stack the dishwasher by herself. Grandad came out to help.

'Grandad it's your birthday. You shouldn't be doing stuff in the kitchen.'

'I just wanted a little word,' he said.

'Go on then. I'm all ears.'

'How long have you and Luke been going out?'

She thought for a moment. 'About two years. Why?'

'Isn't it about time you got married or moved in together. He's such a lovely lad. Good job as well. Trainee solicitor. Oh, you probably think I'm a nosey old bugger but me and your Gran would like to see you settled.'

'Thanks Grandad.' Amy hugged him. If only he'd known it was the last thing she wanted to hear

After her grandparents went home, Amy wanted to be on her own. She didn't want to spend the rest of the evening with Luke. He would want to talk about her resignation at McCauleys. He knew she hadn't told her parents yet, so he would wait until they were on their own. So predictable.

As if on cue, her parents said goodnight and left them alone.

'Tell me about your resignation letter. Did you hand it in?' He couldn't wait to ask her. 'I hope you had second thoughts.'

'No, I didn't. I gave it in, but I've been offered a promotion if I stay on.'

Luke smiled. 'And are you?'

'Yes.'

'That's great news, Amy. So, what next? A new post at McCauleys. Wow! Well done you. We must celebrate.'

'Look Luke, I don't want to talk about it right now. OK?'

'Sorry darling.' He put his arms round her.

She pushed him away.

'I'm going to bed. I haven't had much sleep.'

'Understandable. Promotion eh?'

Amy stared at him. At that moment she wanted Ben. She wanted Ben now. She wanted excitement.

'See you tomorrow then?' He tried to kiss her, but she turned her face away.

It was about a week later that Luke said he thought she had been working too hard. She rarely saw him now. He believed it was work load.

'In two week's time I start my new job. It's all busy busy,' she told him. It was. She often went back to Ben's after work, for snatched moments of passion even when he was involved in other things on the same evening.

'How's everything going?' Luke was always interested in anything she did.

'Really well. I won't be desk-bound soon. I shall be meeting people, chatting, working away sometimes. Cool.'

'That's great, but Amy I hardly see you these days. I'm missing you.'

'Sorry.'

'Can we go out for a bite on Saturday? You won't be working then will you?'

'All right.' She had to say yes. It was a horrible situation. She would tell him the truth on Saturday. She had to stop pretending to him and to the family.

Once the family got over the news of the break up, she absolutely knew they would love Ben. He was a charmer and would instantly win them over, even Grandad.

On Saturday, Pizza Express in Cornmarket Street was busy.

'Lucky I booked,' said Luke.

They were sitting opposite each other and Luke was smiling, while Amy was trying to avoid his eyes.

Olives and bread arrived, and pizzas had been ordered. Luke began eating. Amy sat still. He stopped eating and looked at her across the table.

'Amy, I've got something to tell you, the reason I brought you here. I haven't been seeing you much lately and I realised how much you meant to me. You are part of my life and I love you. I think you should move in with me.

She put her hands over her eyes. Luke's idea was the worst thing that could have happened. If only she could have spoken first.

'No. I can't do that Luke. I'm sorry.'

'I don't understand. Please tell me this isn't true, Amy.' She could see his eyes were filling with tears.

'Oh, but it is true. You see I'm in love with someone else.'

The days which followed were unbearable. Luke had disappeared. Her parents had adopted a kind of silence, tip-toeing around Amy as if they couldn't face talking to her. When they first heard the news, they told her she was thoughtless and didn't deserve a wonderful chap like Luke. The grandparents were also devastated.

'You two were made for each other,' said Grandad.

'How could you,' said Gran.

Amy didn't care. She loved Ben, not Luke.

'Will you come and meet my parents?' she later asked Ben. She'd told him all about Luke and her family.

'That wouldn't be a good idea,' he said. 'Let them get over your break-up with the lovely Luke. Wait a while. It's too soon.' She'd noticed his lip curling when he mentioned her ex. Jealousy she supposed.

Amy was enjoying her new work on reception at McCauleys. She didn't see much of Ben now she was situated near the entrance, which was a good thing as she was sworn to secrecy over their relationship. She even went to the canteen for lunch now and had made a friend, Molly, who worked on accounts and was about to retire.

They were eating there one lunch-break when Ben walked through the canteen followed by a suited man. He never acknowledged Amy, part of their agreement.

'He's a smart chap that Ben Wilson,' said Molly as the two men disappeared out of sight. 'Lovely house in the Cotswolds. My friend knows him vaguely.'

'Oh.' Amy was stunned.

'Yes. Lovely little boy as well. Think he's about five. Don't think he's married but his partner's a model, according to my friend.'

Amy could hardly speak. Molly must be mistaken.

'I thought he had a flat in Oxford.'

'He does. A one-bedroom so he can be on the job. I heard he takes his bits on the side there.' Molly laughed. 'How the other half lives, eh?'

'Yes.' Amy stood up feeling a sense of unreality. Without a word to Molly, she walked out of the canteen, collected her coat and bag and left the building. She caught the bus and sat there totally numb, her hands clenched. She had Molly's words echoing around her. A jumble of horror in her brain.

Of course, Ben was smart, and she had been a fool. She had lost Luke. Or had she? He was so understanding, and he loved her. He was always there for her. She would go to him. Her parents would treat her normally again. Her grandparents would be over the moon. She would tell him she had made a terrible mistake. She would go to his flat as soon as she knew he would be back from work. Everything would be right again, back to her life as it was. She thought of reporting Ben for sexual harassment. Yes, it was what the cheat deserved, but then she'd suffer as much as him. The painful truth was that she had gone along with him willingly, right from the start. Absolutely. She would never set foot in Macauleys again. No way. She almost missed her stop, her mind working overtime.

JENNY BURRAGE

Amy's mum worked mornings only at the hospital so Amy knew she would be at home already. Her grandad's car was in the drive. Her grandparents lived nearby and often popped round.

As she opened the door, she burst into tears. Her mother came out and put her arm round Amy and led her into the sitting room. Her sobs grew louder as she saw her grandparents. They looked concerned, Grandad's hand over his eyes and Gran's hands twisting in her lap.

'Come on darling sit down. It must have been a shock.'

How did they know? Amy wondered. Nobody knew about Ben and what he had done to her.

'What do you mean, Mum?'

'Luke.'

'Luke? What about him?'

'You don't know?'

'No.'

'He's left the country, gone back to live with his parents in Canada. He couldn't face life here anymore. Thanked us, said we'd been like family to him. He texted me about an hour ago.'

Amy couldn't speak. Tears were flowing again.

'But why were you crying when you came in just now, if it wasn't Luke?'

There was a long silence. Finally, Amy spoke. 'Problems at work. Please don't ask me anymore.' She could see her mum was crying now.

'I'm really sorry. I've messed up badly, haven't I? I'm not with my new boyfriend anymore and now I've lost Luke.'

Grandad came and sat beside her. She nestled against his shoulder.

'We all make mistakes, Amy,' he said.